"Let me show you what it's like to be kissed by a real man."

His voice, which had been hard and uncompromising, deepened to a smoky growl.

The feel of that strong-boned body against hers sent an unwanted message to Kristie's brain. This man was dangerous. Not only that, but he was filling her senses. It was something she could well do without. Even now he was taking control of her body, her mind and everything else sensual.

When his mouth came down on hers it sent a further assault shuddering through her.

And all this happened in the space of a few seconds....

Born in the industrial heart of England, **MARGARET MAYO** now lives in a Staffordshire village. She became a writer by accident, after attempting to write a short story when she was almost forty, and now writing is one of the most enjoyable parts of her life. She combines her hobby of photography with her research.

SURRENDER TO THE MILLIONAIRE

MARGARET MAYO

MISTRESS MATERIAL

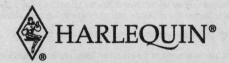

TORONTO • NEW YORK • LONDON
AMSTERDAM • PARIS • SYDNEY • HAMBURG
STOCKHOLM • ATHENS • TOKYO • MILAN • MADRID
PRAGUE • WARSAW • BUDAPEST • AUCKLAND

ISBN 0-373-80620-5

SURRENDER TO THE MILLIONAIRE

First North American Publication 2003.

Copyright © 2003 by Margaret Mayo.

This edition published by arrangement with Harlequin Books S.A.

www.eHarlequin.com

Printed in U.S.A.

PROLOGUE

'TARAH's dead? She can't be!' Kristie refused to accept the news. 'Of course I'll come. Straight away.' And, as she hurtled her car down the motorway to London, she hoped and prayed that it wasn't true. It couldn't be true. Not her darling sister. She had such a zest for life. There was no way in this world that it could have been snuffed out at such a young age.

Twenty-five was nothing—it was the beginning of life. Their parents had died, both of them, in an avalanche when they were skiing in Norway. They'd been in their fifties and even then it had been hard to accept. But Tarah, her dearest sister. 'No, *no, no!*'

Her keening voice filled the car and she shook her head. She had to stay calm while she drove, and somehow she managed to convince herself that it was all a mistake, that it wasn't her sister who had died; it was someone else.

At the hospital she couldn't fool herself any longer.

'We did our best,' said the surgeon sorrowfully, 'but it wasn't enough. The only consolation is that her baby is OK.'

But Kristie didn't care about the baby. It was her sister she mourned.

'Do you want to see him?'

She shook her head. Why couldn't the baby have died and not Tarah? Why was life so unfair? Tears poured down her cheeks.

'I think you should.'

'Whatever you say.' Still in shock, Kristie allowed herself to be led away from her sister's bedside to the nursery. Baby Broderick lay fast asleep, a sweet little angel dressed in blue. And he looked so much like Tarah that a fresh flood of tears erupted. When they asked her whether she would be taking the baby she couldn't find it in her heart to refuse. It wasn't his fault that he'd been left motherless— *and fatherless*!

Kristie had sympathised with Tarah when she had rung to tell her that Radford had dumped her. But when, a week or two later, she had told her that she was pregnant but wasn't going to tell him because he'd always said that he didn't like children and didn't want a family, she had been furious.

'You can't do that,' she'd said. 'He's the father; he's responsible. You can't bring the child up on your own, not without financial help. He owes you that, at least.'

But Tarah had been adamant, and now Tarah was dead. And all because of this man. Kristie had never met him and didn't want to meet him, because she knew that if she did she would kill him.

She had adopted Jake and made him her own and although it had been a struggle, trying to make a living as a single parent, she had managed.

CHAPTER ONE

THE house was invisible from the main road. Kristie had passed this spot many times without realising that the property lurked beyond the ivy-covered walls and the dense woodland.

It was an interesting building—low and wide, looking as though it had been added to over the centuries, resulting in an eclectic mixture of styles and brickwork. And inside it was even more interesting. Kristie had expected a showpiece, each room beautifully furnished while looking as though they were never used. But it wasn't like that. Yes, there were some fine pieces of furniture, but there was also an everyday feel about the place. A newspaper left here, a book there, a jacket slung over the back of a chair. All sorts of little things that showed it was a house well lived in.

'Felicity would like a summer wedding, wouldn't you, darling?'

Kristie turned as a stunningly beautiful girl entered the room in a wheelchair. She had glossy dark hair and most attractive grey eyes. Kristie couldn't help staring and her heart went out to her. It was tragic. Why? How? And yet the girl herself smiled cheerfully.

'The beginning of June, on my birthday. I can't think of anything more perfect.'

'Darling, this is Kristie Swift, the lady I told you about.'

'The one who's going to arrange everything for me?' Felicity wheeled her chair up to Kristie and held out her hand. 'You come highly recommended and you've no idea what a relief it will be for my mother to have everything

7

taken off her hands. She flaps, poor dear.' But it was said in the softest of voices and with an impish smile that made her look like a young girl, whereas Kristie knew for a fact that she'd just had her thirtieth birthday.

'Isn't my brother here yet?' Felicity asked as she whirled back towards the window, peering out at the long drive.

'He's on his way,' affirmed her mother. 'He shouldn't be long. Let's have a drink while we're waiting, shall we?' And to Kristie, 'Felicity's father died several years ago and my son always takes charge on occasions such as this. I don't know what I'd do without him.' Mrs Mandervell-Smythe was an exceedingly well-groomed woman with iron-grey hair and skin that was hardly lined.

'You'd have to find yourself another man,' suggested Felicity cheekily. 'There's no shortage of offers.'

'But no one who fills your father's shoes.'

'Nor is there ever likely to be,' Felicity conceded. 'Daddy was a rare breed. But I do wish you'd find someone, Mummy. I hate seeing you so alone. Hurrah, here he is at last.' Excitedly, Felicity turned her chair and sped out of the room.

Mrs Mandervell-Smythe smiled indulgently. 'As you can tell, Felicity loves her brother very much. He lives and works in London so she doesn't see much of him.'

Kristie heard Felicity's enthusiastic greeting and the rumble of a man's voice. When he entered the room behind his sister his eyes alighted on Kristie instantly. It was like being zapped by a laser gun—a stunning blow to her whole body, making her breath catch in her throat and her heart miss a few beats.

Then his attention turned to his mother and while he was greeting her Kristie studied him. He was by far the most aggressively handsome man she had ever seen—very much like his sister, with the same black hair and intense dark grey eyes. The sort of man who stood out in a crowd, not simply because he was tall and good-looking, but because of an innate charisma. It was like a body magnetism from which Kristie couldn't withdraw. It sucked in her breath and rooted her to the spot.

He turned to her now, his mother introducing him. 'This is Kristie Swift, who's hopefully going to organise Felicity's wedding. Kristie, meet my son, Radford.'

'Brave lady,' he said, with a dazzling white smile. 'My sister is well known for changing her mind.'

Kristie wasn't listening. Radford. Radford Mandervell-Smythe. In an instant Kristie's feelings changed. Radford Smythe. Or Radford Smith, as her sister had insisted on calling him. It had to be the same man. Radford was an uncommon name. In fact, she couldn't remember hearing of anyone else of that name. The smile that was trembling on her lips faded. In fact, her whole face froze and she couldn't even bring herself to touch his outstretched hand.

'Is something wrong?' he asked, his gaze narrowing, his eyes penetrating hers.

'Er, no, nothing,' she managed to stammer. This was unbelievable. She had wanted to meet this man, to see for herself what type of a guy he was, to give him a piece of her mind. But now that the moment was here she was numb.

'You've gone very pale,' remarked his mother with some concern. 'Are you not feeling well? Sit down, please. I'll send for some water.'

'I'm all right,' insisted Kristie, pulling herself together. 'I don't know what came over me.' At least there was nothing she could tell this family. Not yet.

'My brother has this effect on all women,' giggled Felicity.

'Flick!' reprimanded her mother.

But Kristie's thoughts were running deep and she didn't hear. Someone brought in a jug of water and she tried to pour herself a glass but her hands were trembling so much that it spilled over on to the tray.

'Allow me,' came Radford's cool voice, and she had to suffer him standing close while he filled the glass. He was a virile, good-looking man with a powerful masculinity that haunted her senses. She could see why her sister had fallen in love with him. It was impossible not to feel the magnetic pull of his sexuality.

'Drink up,' he urged, folding her still trembling hand around the glass and helping her lift it to her mouth.

Kristie wanted to push him away. She wanted to be anywhere except here in this room with this man who had—

'I said drink. What the hell's wrong with you?' he asked harshly.

'Radford!' exclaimed his mother. 'That's no way to talk to—'

'The woman's shot to pieces,' he retorted. 'She's certainly not fit to organise my sister's wedding. Where the hell did you get her from?' His grey eyes were utterly cold and condemning as they looked down at her.

'She comes highly recommended,' announced Felicity. 'Michelle used her when she got married.'

'Hmph!' he snorted. 'All I can say is Michelle has no taste.'

'Leave the poor girl alone,' insisted his mother. 'Come and sit down, Radford. It's probably you who's making her on edge. You can be extremely overpowering, just like your father.'

'I've done nothing, for pity's sake,' he flared.

'Even so, give Kristie some room.'

Kristie began to feel embarrassed and with a huge effort pulled herself together, drinking more of the water before setting the glass back down on the tray. 'I'm sorry. I don't know what came over me.' Which was a lie, but how could she tell Mrs Mandervell-Smythe what a swine her son was?

'Don't worry about it,' said the older woman. 'Are you up to carrying on with the wedding arrangements?'

'She looks to me as though she ought to go home and lie down,' growled Radford, eyeing her suspiciously.

Kristie glared but said nothing.

Felicity giggled again, seeming to find the whole thing highly amusing.

'I'm fine now,' said Kristie quietly, while knowing that with Radford Smythe in the room she would be unable to concentrate on a word that was said. She hated this man with every fibre of her being.

She could hear her sister's voice telling her that she had met the most gorgeous man in the whole world. 'He's unbelievably handsome and incredibly sexy, Kristie. Wait till you meet him. You'll see what I mean.'

Kristie did see. He was all Tarah had raved about. All and more. He was the sort of man who drew you to him whether you wished it or not. He had a magnetism that was incredibly strong and Kristie expected that few women resisted him.

Her sister had a broken marriage behind her and had moved down to London to start a new life. She had sworn off men for ever—until she met Radford Smythe. 'I tease him and call him Smith,' she told Kristie. 'He doesn't like it, not one little bit. He actually has a double-barrelled name but he never uses it. He runs the family publishing business. His father's dead and his mother lives somewhere near Stratford. Small world, isn't it?'

Too small. This house was only a few miles from where Kristie lived. She suddenly realised that Mrs Mandervell-

Smythe was speaking to her and she hadn't heard a word that was said.

After that Kristie was careful to pay attention to their requests, making suggestions of her own, jotting everything down in her notebook ready to feed into her computer later. Some day she promised to buy herself a laptop. With the right program she could fill everything in as her clients spoke and it would save an awful lot of time.

Halfway through proceedings, coffee and biscuits were brought in. Kristie felt her nerves jangle again when Radford passed her the plate and his eyes met hers in a deliberate questioning stare. And then he smiled—the sort of smile that would have melted the heart of most girls. Kristie managed a grimace, unable to bring herself to smile properly, and took a couple of shortbreads.

'You're looking better,' he said softly.

Kristie nodded.

'We'll talk later and you can tell me exactly what made you feel faint.'

'I don't think so,' answered Kristie smartly. 'I have another pressing engagement after this one.'

'Perhaps you're doing too much?'

'And is that any business of yours?' The moment the words were out Kristie wished she hadn't spoken them. She saw his mother look at her sharply and Felicity's quickened interest. But most of all she saw Radford's face go granite hard, his eyes darkening to a sooty black. And when he straightened he towered above her like a menacing angel, nostrils flared, his mouth grim and straight.

Kristie nibbled a biscuit and sipped her coffee, aware that she was now the subject of much curiosity. She would have liked to leave, get away from the detestable Radford Smythe. But there was still a lot to sort out and he was insistent on having a say in every aspect of the arrangements.

Even when they moved out into the garden where the wedding was going to be held he dominated the conversation.

'I think the ceremony itself should take place just here,' Kristie said, standing at a spot on the lawn about twenty yards away from the house, directly in line with the drawing room where three arched floor to ceiling windows opened out on to the garden. 'With a covered walkway—just in case it rains.' They all knew that in an English June there was every chance of rain. 'And here—' she spread her hands and did a twirl '—would be a huge flat dais, with perhaps Greek or Doric columns and a cover of silk, all swathed with ribbons to match the bridesmaids' dresses and flowers, and plenty of greenery.'

She was conscious of Radford's eyes on her all the time and more than a couple of hours passed before they had talked through everything. Kristie felt relief as she finally got to her feet. 'I'll be in touch,' she said, looking directly at Mrs Mandervell-Smythe, avoiding any eye contact whatsoever with her son.

'I'll see you out,' he said, much to her dismay.

Kristie wanted to object but felt it would be impolite to draw further attention to herself. He touched his hand to her elbow as he led her to the door. Was this to stop her running away before he'd had the chance to question her odd behaviour? wondered Kristie. It was a million to one chance that they'd met like this—a million to one chance she could have done without.

Admittedly, she'd wanted to meet this man and give him a piece of her mind, but not like this, not in front of his mother and a prospective client to boot. What she had to say to him was strictly private.

When she reached her car he was still following. She opened the door but he put his hand on it before she could get in. 'Suppose you tell me what that was all about?'

'What?' she asked sharply.

'That little display of hysterics.'

'I'm not used to brothers of the bride putting in their two pennyworth,' she prevaricated. Damn him, why couldn't he keep out of her way? Her memories were bad enough without him adding to them.

'Is that so?' Dark brows rose. 'And it upset you that much? I think not. I think there's more to it.'

'You can think what you like,' she retorted. 'I don't need to answer to you. Will you please let me go? I'm running late for my next appointment.'

'How about lunch?'

'Not on your life!'

'I wasn't inviting you,' he drawled, with a cold glitter in his eyes. 'I meant what are you going to do about lunch? You can't run from one job to another without eating. If that's your general practice it's no wonder you feel ill.'

Kristie groaned inwardly. She was making a thorough fool of herself. Thankfully, he took his hand away from the door and she was able to slide inside and start the engine.

But she was not free of him yet. He lowered his head and looked through the still open doorway. 'Goodbye, Kristie Swift. Maybe the next time we meet you'll be in a better frame of mind.'

Never! And she was about to tell him so when she thought better of it. She smiled weakly instead. 'Goodbye, Mr Mandervell-Smythe.'

It wasn't until she was out of his sight and out of the gates that Kristie was able to breathe a sigh of relief. But even so her hands were trembling so much that she stopped the car and took several deep steadying breaths before she could continue. She used her mobile to cancel her next appointment and then headed straight home. Concentrating on work was out of the question.

Kristie lived in a smart townhouse on the outskirts of Warwick. It had three bedrooms, a fairly large lounge and a kitchen, and she loved it. There was no garden at the front but a long patch of lawn at the back. She made herself a strong cup of coffee and sat at her breakfast bar sipping it, looking out at the grass, which was badly in need of mowing. She would do it in a minute. The physical act of pushing the mower would help rid her mind of the aggression that was steadily building to a crescendo.

She had never imagined for one moment that she would meet Radford Smythe. Tarah had raved about him. 'He's fabulously sexy, the most fantastic man in the whole world,' she had enthused. Kristie had been sceptical because Tarah had said the same about her husband—and look what had happened there.

Tarah had been two years older than Kristie, headstrong and fanatical, throwing herself wholeheartedly into whatever hobby or relationship took her fancy. Kristie had always been the one who rescued her when she ended up hurt or disillusioned. It had been like that all their lives, even at school.

When Tarah met Bryan Broderick, the man she married, she had been head over heels in love for all of six months, until she found out that he had been seeing another woman. Kristie had again been the one who had picked up the pieces. Tarah's decision to move to London and create a new life for herself had been met with dismay from both Kristie and their parents, but nothing they could say had made any difference.

And now she was dead!

And all because of a man named Radford Mandervell-Smythe.

CHAPTER TWO

'WHAT do you think was wrong with Miss Swift?' Radford asked as he walked back into the room.

'I think you overwhelmed her,' giggled Felicity. 'She was fine until you came on the scene. Is that a first, someone swooning at your feet?'

'Don't be ridiculous,' he snorted. 'It had nothing to do with me.'

'I think the poor girl's overworked,' announced his mother. 'She's dreadfully thin and pale.'

Radford nodded. 'I don't think we should give her the job. I think I ought to go and see her and tell her that—'

'No!' insisted Mrs Mandervell-Smythe. 'I'd like to talk to her some more. She was very enthusiastic and certainly full of excellent ideas. It would be a pity to dismiss her before we're absolutely sure she's not up to the job.'

Radford privately doubted the woman could do it. She'd gone completely to pieces when he spoke to her and that was no good for business. He certainly had no intention of keeping out of her way. He'd be here to make sure that every aspect of his sister's wedding went without a hitch.

He knew that was what his mother was paying Kristie Swift for, but he didn't trust her. For some reason she had taken a dislike to him. Unusual, to say the least, because he was more used to fighting women off, but he had to admit that he didn't find her in the least attractive either.

So why, he asked himself a short while later, did the image of her pale but interesting face, framed by striking red hair, keep inserting itself into his mind's eye? For some strange reason he couldn't dismiss her from his mind. She had the most unusual light green eyes, very wide and very beautiful, and he wondered what colour they went when she was being made love to.

He shook his head and dismissed the thought. It was of little consequence; it was something that was never likely to happen.

Kristie gulped her coffee and squeezed the mug so hard between her palms that it was a wonder it didn't shatter. For five years she had carried a massive hostility in her heart for this faceless man. She had tried to bury her feelings, told herself that there was no point in harbouring such malevolent thoughts when she was never likely to meet him. And to a degree she had been successful.

But now her pain and distress flooded back to the surface with a vengeance and she knew that if he was going to attend every discussion it was going to make her situation untenable. Maybe she ought to opt out of this job? It was but a fleeting thought. It wasn't Kristie's way. She met all problems head-on, and that was all he was—a problem. A mighty big one, admittedly, but now that she knew the situation Kristie felt sure she could handle it.

She wouldn't let him see again that he upset her but she would find a way to make very sure that he got his due punishment. Quite how she didn't know, but she was very definite in her mind that he wouldn't get away with what he had done.

Her phone rang but she ignored it. Her head ached, her heart ached; she didn't want to talk to anyone. But then came that deep, gravelly male voice over her answerphone. 'Miss Swift, it's Radford Smythe here.'

As if she couldn't tell!

'I have a message for you from my mother.'

It was as though he was in the same room and it sent an unfortunate shiver down her spine. She couldn't forget those unfathomable dark grey eyes, or that harshly boned face.

'She would like to see you again; there's something she forgot. She'll be at home this evening.'

That was it. The connection was cut. It sounded more like an order than anything else. Kristie's hackles rose and she jumped to her feet. She'd ring the darn man back and tell him it was out of the question. But before she could even get to the phone it rang again. She snatched it up angrily. 'If that's you, Smythe, with yet another request, you can—'

'Kristie?'

'Oh, Paul, I'm sorry.'

'Who did you think I was?'

'It doesn't matter. Someone I met today.'

'Someone you don't like by the sound of things. Shall I come and soothe your ravaged breast?'

Kristie laughed. 'It's not that bad. He simply wound me up the wrong way.'

'It's been ages since I saw you.'

'I have work to do.'

'That's always your excuse,' he grumbled. 'I'm beginning to think your business means more to you than I do.'

'My business puts a roof over my head and food in my mouth, you know that.'

'Which I could do if you'd let me,' he said persuasively.

'Paul,' she groaned, 'don't start that again. We're just friends; let's keep it that way.' She had known Paul for over twelve months now and, although she was very fond of him, she wanted to take things slowly. She wasn't yet ready for a committed relationship.

'I'd nevertheless like to come.'

'I'm busy,' she said softly, regretfully. He had no idea what it was like running a one-man business. When she had set up as a wedding co-ordinator she had thought it would be relatively easy. She hadn't realised all the hard work and often long hours that were involved. But she loved her job and wouldn't change it for the world.

'Soon, then?' he asked.

'Soon,' she promised. 'I'll ring you.'

No sooner had she put down the phone than thoughts of Radford Smythe swept back into her mind. She was swiftly discovering that he was not a man who could be ignored, and it was easy to see why her sister had fallen so madly in love with him.

But she wasn't alone with her thoughts for long. The door burst open and Jake came rushing in. 'Mummy, Mummy, look what I've painted for you.'

Chloe walked in behind him. 'We've had to run all the way home from school. I warned him you might not be in, but—'

'Guess who it is.' Jake hopped from foot to foot in his excitement.

'Your teacher?' she suggested hopefully. The stick figure with the fuzzy orange hair and bright red mouth could have been anyone.

'Course not, it's you.'

'I know, sweetheart. I was teasing.' She picked Jake up and hugged him, twirling him around while he squealed with delight. 'I love it.'

The rest of Kristie's day was spent with her young son. Chloe was her live-in babysitter and normally she kept Jake out of the way until Kristie's work was finished. But today Jake was exactly what she needed to take her mind off Radford Smythe. And she certainly had no intention of going to see his mother, not this evening anyway.

Who did he think he was, issuing orders like that? Her sister had obviously looked at him through blinkered eyes, had seen only that he was devilishly handsome and magnificently sexy, ignored the fact that he lacked basic good manners. Well she wasn't going to ignore it—it only added to her already rock-bottom opinion of him.

Kristie waited until the next morning before phoning Mrs Mandervell-Smythe, only to be told that she wasn't in. But Mr Radford Smythe was in, if he could help.

About to tell whoever it was who had answered the phone that she would like to leave a message, a voice that was becoming all too familiar sounded in her ear.

'Kristie Swift?'

She swallowed hard. 'That's right.' She hadn't even thought that he might still be there. She had believed, in fact she had hoped, that he'd gone back to London. She didn't want anything more to do with this man. Because if she did she would pull no punches in telling him exactly what she thought of him.

'Where were you last night?' he asked brusquely.

'I beg your pardon?' Her hackles were rising already.

'I asked you to come for a further consultation.'

Kristie's chin lifted. 'You didn't ask, you ordered, and I don't take kindly to that sort of language. But, as a matter of fact,' she went on, hearing his hiss of disbelief, 'I had something far more important to do.' Little Jake was the focus of her life, more important than anything or anyone else. 'Except that you didn't wait to hear.'

There was a pause before he answered, a pause when she knew he was trying to control himself. She didn't care. He deserved to be treated badly.

'So when would it be convenient for you to call?' he asked, his voice full of dry sarcasm.

'Perhaps this afternoon, about three-thirty,' she suggested.

'I'll let my mother know.'

'Tell me,' she said, before she could stop herself. 'Is it you or your mother who calls the shots? I really would like to know who I'm dealing with.'

There was a long pause and Kristie began to feel uncomfortable. She ought not to have spoken to him like that. He had been doubtful before whether she was up to doing the job, now he must be sure. She had probably burnt her bridges altogether.

'I'm sorry,' she said quickly. 'That was very rude of me. I'll see your mother at three-thirty.' And she put down the phone.

She breathed out a long, deflating sigh. It was wrong to show her hatred of Radford Smythe at this stage. She couldn't afford to lose this commission. She had never realised before Jake came into her life how much it cost to keep a small child. And moving from her flat into a house with a huge mortgage hadn't helped. Chloe's share of the housekeeping costs helped, reduced in return for her babysitting and sometimes office services, but she still needed to work hard to keep her head above water.

Kristie kept herself busy for the next few hours—she even managed to forget Radford Smythe. But all too soon three-thirty approached and as she drove towards their country estate her heart began to beat unevenly. She didn't want to be faced with this man again, not in the presence of his mother and sister. He sent her all jittery, and it had to be because of the hatred that lived in her soul.

But wishing him away had no effect whatsoever. The twelve-foot high gates swung open as she approached and Radford himself met her at the door. He had clearly been awaiting her arrival. 'Thank you for coming,' he said drily, grey eyes penetrating hers with such intensity that it felt as though he was looking into her soul. Or at the very least trying to read her mind. 'Do come in.'

He wore a white open-necked shirt and dark green casual trousers, and he looked totally relaxed. There was even a tiny smile playing at the corners of his mouth. She felt distinctly uncomfortable. It was those probing eyes that did it. Beautiful eyes admittedly, with long thick lashes, but they saw too much. She had a feeling no secret was safe from this man.

He stood back and allowed her to enter and she hovered in the vast hall while he closed the door and then followed him into the room where she had spoken to his mother the day before. It was empty.

'Unfortunately, my mother's not home yet,' he said, still with that annoying little smile.

He was enjoying this, but she sure as hell wasn't. All good intentions fled. 'And you didn't think to tell me? You've let me waste my time?' Fury flashed in her green eyes and she felt like turning round and storming out.

'I didn't think it was a waste,' he answered, his tone even. 'I wanted to see you again.'

'Why?' she demanded hotly. 'To confirm your opinion that I'm not up to the job?' She stared straight into his face, virtually daring him to agree.

'You didn't exactly instil me with confidence,' he answered, his eyes unblinking on hers. 'Why was that, I wonder?'

Kristie ignored the question. 'What time are you expecting your mother?'

Wide shoulders shrugged expressively.

'So what am I doing here?' And why was she suddenly beginning to feel nervous? She had the strangest feeling that he had designs on her. As if she would ever, *ever*, contemplate going out with this man. He had a lot to learn.

'My sister will be joining us shortly,' he announced. 'You needn't fear, your time won't be entirely wasted. The wedding plans will be discussed. Why don't you sit down?'

Kristie didn't want to sit—she wanted to leave, come back again when his mother was here and he wasn't, but to do so would provoke all sorts of awkward questions. So she perched herself on a chair as far away from him as she could without it looking as though she was deliberately avoiding him.

Radford remained standing, leaning back against the edge of a solid oak table on which stood a vase of roses which spilt their heady perfume into the room, his ankles crossed, his arms folded across a magnificently broad chest and his head tilted to one side. 'Is it men in general you don't like or just me?'

Kristie allowed her eyebrows to arch delicately. 'What makes you think I don't like you?'

'Was it a bad experience?' he asked, ignoring her question.

'You could say that.'

'It doesn't mean all men are the same.'

'No?'

'Perhaps you'd like to talk about it?'

'Not on your life,' she tossed back. There was a whole lot of stuff she wanted to say to this man but not at this moment, not when they were likely to be interrupted. What she had to say was very personal indeed—and it most definitely wouldn't be polite!

It might be interesting, though, to find out exactly what sort of a man he was. Sexy and woman-appealing, without a doubt, but what was he like deep down? Why had he dumped Tarah? Perhaps she could find out how his mind worked? Perhaps he was the love 'em and leave 'em type? Not that she was likely to let herself get into that kind of situation. But perhaps during conversation she could find out how many women there had been in his life, whether he'd been serious about any of them, whether he was married, and if not why not.

'It still leaves the question—why did you go to pieces when you saw me yesterday?'

CHAPTER THREE

KRISTIE SWIFT was the most intriguing female Radford had ever met. Since seeing her yesterday he had been unable to get her out of his mind. She was feisty, she was beautiful, and for some unknown reason she had taken an instant dislike to him—to the extent that she had almost passed out. Perhaps he reminded her of someone who had let her down badly. But if that was the case why couldn't she say so? Why ignore his questions? Even now she prevaricated.

'You think it was because of you that I felt faint?' she asked, widening her lovely green eyes and lifting her chin in a proud gesture which he found truly enchanting.

'It was the impression you gave.'

'Then you're being very conceited. Why would a perfect stranger blow me over like that?'

'You tell me,' he said. 'I know only what I saw. The moment my name was mentioned you lost all your colour.'

'You're imagining things,' she retorted, but Radford knew what he had seen and he wouldn't be happy until he had found out the reason why. But he could wait. There was no rush. He moved closer towards her and sat down. He felt her inching away—nothing discernible, but the feeling was there all the same. And he was annoyed by the action. It wasn't the usual effect he had on the opposite sex. It didn't sit easily on his shoulders.

'Would you like a cup of tea?' he asked. 'Or coffee?' It was difficult to keep an edge from his voice.

'Nothing, thank you,' she answered coolly. 'Does your sister know that I'm here?'

'She knows. How long have you been arranging other people's weddings?' He wanted to know everything there was to know about this girl. What made her tick. Where she lived. Who she lived with. He had already noticed that she didn't wear a wedding ring, but he wanted to know whether there was a man in her life.

'Five years—almost. Why?' she questioned fiercely. 'Does it make a difference? I am fully qualified, I assure you, and I'll be happy to provide the names of previous clients.'

Heavens, she was prickly. Maybe he ought to carry out a few checks. His mother had taken her at face value, but he felt sure she hadn't seen this side of Kristie Swift. His sister's wedding was very important to him. Life had dealt her a raw hand and meeting and falling in love with Daniel Fielding was a wonderful happening. He wanted her wedding day to be perfect, totally hassle-free. But if this uptight woman was going to fly off the handle at every little hurdle then she certainly wasn't the right person for the job.

'I think that might be a good idea,' he said. 'One recommendation by Felicity's friend is hardly a good testimony. I'll drop by your office for the list.'

'I'll post it,' she snapped, 'if it's so important to you. Have you spoken to Michelle yourself?'

'I don't know her,' he snarled, his patience wearing thin. 'She's my sister's friend, not mine.'

'Don't you think that Felicity's the main person in all of this?' demanded Kristie, her eyes flashing furiously. 'Shouldn't she have a say? And if she's happy, then I think you should butt out.'

Lord, had she really said that? Kristie's blood ran hot and fluid through her veins and she wished herself anywhere but here. But before Radford could answer the sound of clapping came from the doorway. 'Well said, Kristie.

It's about time my uppity brother got some of his own treatment.'

The change in Radford was dramatic. His scowl turned to an instant smile and as his sister wheeled her chair towards him he spoke to her tenderly. 'You weren't supposed to hear that, cherub.'

'I think the whole house heard. You two weren't pulling any punches, were you? What's wrong, darling brother of mine, doesn't Miss Swift conform to the way the female sex usually treats you?'

'I merely wanted to check her credentials,' he reproved softly. 'It's the normal way to conduct business.'

'And it's normal for someone to tell you to "butt out"? Wonderful, Kristie.'

Kristie gave an uncomfortable smile and wondered how much of the conversation Felicity had heard. It didn't put her in a good light, that was for sure.

Radford stroked a light hand over his sister's jet-black hair. 'I'm glad you found our little altercation amusing.'

Felicity's infectious laughter rang out. 'It's going to be fun having Kristie around. Don't let him harass you,' she said, switching her attention. 'Michelle couldn't sing your praises highly enough. We don't need testimonials.'

'I think maybe we should get on with the business,' said Kristie. The sooner she was out of this house the better.

But her torture didn't end as swiftly as she would have liked. Mrs Mandervell-Smythe returned an hour later and she was forced to go through everything all over again. It was hard to believe that Radford was the same person. He was full of charm and courtesy, listening to her proposals, nodding, agreeing, only occasionally questioning—like when she mentioned creating individual pieces of jewellery. He must have been like this when her sister first met him. The perfect English gentleman. No hint of his darker side.

It was no wonder Tarah had fallen head over heels in love. But how swiftly his temper was aroused, how easily he condemned.

Kristie was glad when the agreement was finally signed and she could take her leave, but even then Radford insisted on walking her out to her car. 'There's no need,' she told him testily at the door, but still he accompanied her.

'Are you satisfied now that I can do the job properly?' she asked huffily as she unlocked the door. Her old red Ford was definitely the poor relation. His black Mercedes sat one side of it and his mother's Jaguar the other. She expected some comment, but none was forthcoming.

'I guess I'll have to be,' he said shortly. 'One slip up, though, and you'll be out. Is that understood? I won't have Felicity upset. She's suffered enough.'

'Don't worry. Everything will run as smoothly as silk,' she assured him. 'And you don't need to hang around to make sure. You can go back to London with complete peace of mind.'

'I wish,' he said, so quietly that she almost didn't hear. But she didn't retaliate. She slid into her car instead and shot off so quickly that gravel spurted beneath her wheels. She saw Radford's look of distaste through her rear view mirror.

The house was empty when Kristie arrived home. Chloe had taken Jake to a friend's birthday party so she had the luxury of being completely alone. Changing into a pair of old jeans and a T-shirt, she pushed her mower furiously up and down the lawn, muttering to herself all the time, vainly attempting to expurgate Radford from her mind.

She was hot and sweaty and on her way to take a shower when the doorbell rang. Snatching the door open, Kristie was ready to send away whichever salesman was calling with a flea in his ear. They were a nuisance. If it wasn't double-glazing it was guttering, or tree-felling, or any of a number of things that they assured her would improve her property.

Her harsh words stuck in her throat when she saw Radford Smythe. Hell, what was he doing here? Hadn't he said everything there was to be said? Or was it for the list of previous clients? Was he still not convinced that she would do a good job?

'What do you want?' she asked curtly.

'Have I called at a bad time?'

No time would be a good time where this man was concerned. 'I was about to take a shower,' she informed him icily.

'Don't let me stop you. I'll wait.'

With an insolence she found annoying, he slowly looked her up and down, starting with the shabby trainers on her feet, working his way over her slender hips and flat stomach. Tension ran through her, especially when his eyes rested much longer than Kristie was happy with on her breasts, which had unfortunately peaked beneath the too-tight T-shirt. It was one she kept specifically for gardening.

And he carried on his inspection right up to her hair, which she had scraped unbecomingly back in a band to keep it out of the way while she worked. Lastly, his eyes returned to her face.

His was totally devoid of expression. She had no idea what he was thinking—probably something along the lines that she didn't look a fit person to co-ordinate his sister's wedding and he'd made a fatal mistake in letting his mother agree.

You're not waiting here, she answered silently. Not on your life. She could just imagine herself standing naked under the steaming jets while he paced impatiently below.

The very thought sent a surge of unwanted heat over her skin. She didn't trust this man an inch.

In fact, she wouldn't put it past him to follow her upstairs and covertly watch as she showered. Or maybe not even secretly, he could well do it openly. He seemed to her to be the type of guy who did and said exactly what he wanted regardless of protocol or circumstances.

Oh, lord, why was she thinking along these lines? He wasn't interested in her, not one little bit. He didn't even want her to plan his sister's wedding. This was probably why he was here—to say that her services were no longer required.

'I'd rather get whatever it is you want over and done with,' she insisted.

Radford inclined his head. 'May I come in then?'

Reluctantly, Kristie stood back. She hadn't realised quite what a big man he was until he stepped into her hall. His mother's house was so spacious that he hadn't filled the room with his presence—well, not quite. But here—she felt as though he had breathed in every little bit of air and left nothing for her. He dominated the tiny space and she moved quickly into her living room, one corner of which served as her office.

'So why are you here?' she asked when he said nothing, when he simply looked around him with interest. It was a fairly minimalist room in natural colours. She hated clutter, not that it was always possible to avoid when Jake was playing with his toys, but she kept it tidy and was glad of this now.

'I was curious.'

Kristie frowned. 'About what?'

'You.'

'And that gives you the right to intrude on my personal space?' she asked incredulously. 'I don't think so, Mr

Smythe. If you're not here on business then I'd like you to leave.' And that was putting it politely. The nerve of the man. This wasn't protecting his sister's interests, this was satisfying his own curiosity.

And yet, angry as she was, she couldn't dismiss his innate sexuality. It emanated from him like a strong, heady perfume, filling the air around him, making him alarmingly attractive. She swore silently as the thought hit her. Please God, she prayed, don't let me be attracted to this man. Don't let me fall into his trap the same way Tarah did.

Unconsciously, she backed away. Radford frowned. 'I don't bite,' he snarled, 'and I have no intention of leaving. You can either take a shower and I'll wait for our talk, or we can do it right now.'

'Now will suit me fine,' she fired. 'What is it you want to know?'

'A little about yourself.'

Kristie gave a quick frown. 'Why? What's that got to do with anything?'

'I'm curious, that's all.'

'You mean plain nosy,' she snapped.

His lips thinned and a cold gleam entered his eyes. 'Politeness costs nothing.'

Immediately Kristie felt ashamed. This was far from the image she normally portrayed. She'd always made an attempt to be cool and calm and professional—except that professionalism had flown out of the window where this man was concerned, swiftly followed by any pretence of tranquillity.

'Tell me,' he said cuttingly, 'exactly what is it that you've got against me?'

Kristie closed her eyes for a moment. This was not the time to discuss the way he had treated Tarah. Chloe and

Jake would be home any minute. In fact, she ought never to have let him in. It had been an insane decision.

'Don't keep denying it,' he snarled.

'Let's just say that there are some types of men I like and some I don't,' she said, swallowing a tight lump in her throat and daring to look him straight in the eye. It was a big mistake. They were rock hard and bored right into her.

'And I belong to the latter group?'

She nodded.

Nostrils flared. 'And you think it's right to categorise someone before you get to know them?'

'I shouldn't have done that,' she admitted. 'I'm sorry. Now will you go?' Lord, it hurt to apologise but if that was what it took to get rid of him then it was worth it.

'You're not getting away that lightly,' he snorted, still with that steely glint in his eye. 'I want to know what this guy did to make you condemn everyone who reminds you of him.'

'Who said it's a certain guy?' she retorted. 'In any case, it's none of your business.'

'Maybe not,' he agreed, 'but it's certainly had a profound effect. Do you have a current boyfriend?'

Kristie glared. 'I refuse to answer any more of your questions. You and I have a strictly business relationship, nothing more. I can't imagine why you're here and I want you to leave.'

'Is this where you work?' he asked, glancing across at the corner of the room where her desk, filing cabinet and bookshelves sat in a tidy huddle.

'It is.'

'It doesn't look very professional.' A deep, disapproving frown scored his brow. 'Don't you have a room you can use as an office?'

'I don't need one,' she answered tightly. 'This suits me fine.'

'I—'

He was interrupted by the sound of Chloe's key in the lock and the next moment the girl's face appeared round the door. 'I saw the car and guessed you had a visitor. I'll go and bath Jake; he's had the time of his life.' Jake looked into the room too but he hung back instead of rushing in to give Kristie her customary hug and a kiss. He was incredibly shy where strangers were concerned, which was as well under the circumstances, thought Kristie. She didn't want to answer any questions about him.

But Radford's curiosity was aroused. 'You share this house?'

Kristie nodded.

'Who's the owner, you or your—er, friend?' He nodded towards the door.

'Me,' she rasped, wishing he wouldn't ask so many questions. 'Mortgages don't come cheap.'

His eyes narrowed. 'So your business isn't exactly flourishing?' Again his eyes flashed disparagingly towards the corner of the room.

It was exactly what he'd like to hear. Any excuse to discredit her. 'It's doing well, thank you, but I can't afford to sit back on my early laurels. It takes a while to get fully established and build a reputation, as you probably know. I imagine you're in business too, Mr Smythe?'

'I run the family business,' he acknowledged.

So he hadn't had to work his way up like most people. No wonder he was overbearingly pompous—he had the world at his feet and clearly thought he could treat people any way he liked. It was time he went.

She moved towards the door. 'I really must take that shower, Mr Smythe. Let me show you out.'

*   *   *

Radford found it difficult to understand Kristie's attitude—
he had never met anyone quite like her. And the more she
appeared to hold some grudge against him the more in-
trigued by her he became, the more determined not to be
summarily dismissed.

'I'm not sure that I'm ready to go yet,' he said crisply.

'What more is there to be said?' she questioned, her
lovely green eyes flashing their displeasure at him. He had
never seen eyes quite so beautiful. They were an extraor-
dinarily pale green with a dark line around the iris which
stopped them from being lost against the very white whites.
They were wide-spaced and sloe-shaped, with extremely
long lashes that, he guessed, would make many a man's
heart flutter. If she cared to use them.

Was she hostile to all men, he wondered, or had he been
singled out for special treatment? There was no way of
knowing. And she hadn't answered his question about
whether there was a man in her life. His quick glance
around the room had revealed no photographs. In fact, he
had never seen a room so devoid of personal possessions.
It was such a plain room that he wondered how she found
pleasure in it. Kristie herself was the only splash of colour.

At his mother's house earlier she had been dressed in a
lime green softly structured suit with a cream blouse. She
had looked the epitome of a successful woman, very self-
confident, very feminine—and utterly desirable. He hated
to admit it but his heart had rumbled within his chest and
he had felt an urge to get to know her better. It was why
he was here. And what a waste of time it had been.

He had been shocked to see her in jeans, not that he
didn't like her in them; he did. They showed off her figure
to perfection, faithfully tracing the curves of her hips and
bottom. His groin ached simply thinking about what lay

underneath. And that T-shirt! Before, he'd only been able to guess at her shape. This revealed all. Her breasts were pert and thrusting, simply asking to be touched.

He gave his head a mental shake, he shouldn't be thinking along these lines, not when she'd made it abundantly clear that she hated the very sight of him. He ought to go, he ought to do as she asked, and yet something still made him want to stay and find out more about this enigmatic girl. She had struck a chord with him that no other woman had.

'I really think that—'

'There's nothing more to be said, Mr Smythe,' she cut in sharply.

'You're a hard woman, Kristie Swift.'

'I need to be.'

'Would you be free to have dinner with me tonight?' The words popped out before he'd even thought about them. But he knew what her answer would be.

'Why?'

She surprised him. He had expected a flat no. 'Does there have to be a reason for a man to ask a beautiful girl out?'

'Yes, when it's you,' she shot back.

He was a fool for hanging around, a fool for coming, even, and his voice was sharp. 'And what is that supposed to mean? Are you suggesting I have an ulterior motive?'

'Actually, yes, I am,' she retorted. 'You want to ply me with questions, and taking me out means there'll be no interruptions and I'll have no escape.'

She was astute, he had to give her that. There was so much he wanted to know about her—especially why she was so hostile towards him, but how was he to do that if she wouldn't co-operate? 'You find it hard to talk to me?'

'I simply see it as none of your business.'

He wanted to take the band out of her hair and let it fall

about her face in a fiery glow. He wanted to touch her, to feel that slender body against his. He wanted to kiss her. Each one of these separate thoughts amazed him. Here was this stroppy woman who had no time for him and yet he wanted her like he had no other. 'I don't take no for an answer easily,' he said.

'You'll be wasting your time.' And as she spoke she opened the front door. 'Goodbye, Mr Smythe.'

'For now,' he said with a faint smile. The urge to kiss her as he squeezed past was so strong that he didn't know how he managed to control himself. She was excitingly sexy, and the scent of her perfume that had intoxicated him earlier still lingered. She was all woman without a doubt— if she would only let go. Getting through to her would be an exercise in extreme patience and tact.

He paused a moment, their bodies but a hair's breadth away, and he looked deeply into her eyes. 'It will be interesting getting to know you, Miss Swift.'

Alarm flickered across her face and he felt the heat of her skin shooting across the space between them. She wanted to move, he knew, but she didn't want to give away the fact that he disturbed her. She stood tall and straight, her chin defiant and her eyes a green blaze.

He would have given anything to know why she was so against him. It was a question he had asked himself numerous times since meeting this delightful creature, but no answer had suggested itself. He couldn't make out whether it was something personal or whether she was dead set against the whole of mankind. What he did know was that it would be infinitely interesting to find out.

It was with intense reluctance that he finally moved. He had expected Kristie to give in first and yell at him to go. He had looked forward to seeing her eyes flash again and her cheeks fill with angry colour, but no, she stood her ground and waited. And now he had no reason to linger. He didn't even feel that he dared give her the lightest of kisses—not if he wanted to build up a relationship.

Kristie slammed the door behind Radford. She couldn't think of one good reason why he had come here, except to find out what sort of a person she really was, whether she was worthy of organising his sister's wedding.

What conclusion had he drawn? She certainly hadn't been very polite and she wondered now whether it had been to her detriment, whether he would advise his mother to find someone else. Damn! She could ill afford to lose business this way. Why hadn't she cast her personal hatred aside and treated him with the professionalism the job deserved?

'Mummy! Mummy!' Jake came bounding downstairs and all thoughts of Radford Smythe fled—until she lay in bed much later that evening.

Nothing then would dismiss him from her mind. He was such an amazingly sexy man that he awoke senses she hadn't felt in a long time, if ever. Senses that she knew were dangerous and should be immediately and permanently dismissed. This was a man she hated with every fibre of her being.

She needed to distance herself from him, but how was she to do that when he insisted on taking part in the wedding arrangements? If only he would leave it to his mother, go back to London and not turn up again until the wedding day. But somehow she had the feeling that he wouldn't do that. He was going to oversee this thing every inch of the way.

He had sensed her antagonism—no, not sensed, he had seen it. She had foolishly allowed her feelings to show, and now he was going to do everything in his power to find out why. Hence the dinner invitation.

Maybe she ought to confront him now and get it over with. On the other hand, it could cost her the job. All she had to do was retain her cool, be polite to him at all times, and do everything else to the best of her ability.

Simple.

CHAPTER FOUR

KRISTIE immersed herself in her work the next morning, deliberately squashing all thoughts of Radford Smythe—until the phone rang and it was his mother.

'Kristie, I need to see you. I've had the most wonderful idea.'

Kristie gave a mental groan. It was usual for there to be lots of interchanges of ideas, lots of alterations to plans, and under normal circumstances she'd have dropped everything and gone over. But not if there was a likelihood of her son being present. She'd had as much of him as she could stomach for the time being. 'I'm very busy, Mrs Mandervell-Smythe. I don't think I could come over right now.'

'I wasn't meaning straight away, dear. Perhaps you could join us for dinner tonight and I'll put my proposal to you then?' And as Kristie hesitated, 'I won't take no for an answer. I think you'll be quite excited by what I have to say.'

How could she refuse? Especially as this was one of the biggest weddings she'd so far been asked to organise. The Mandervell-Smythes were very influential people and no expense was to be spared. It could earn her a tidy sum. Besides, Jake would be in bed by then so she wouldn't miss out on their usual playtime—something that was very important to her.

'What time would you like me to be there?'

'Good girl. Shall we say about seven thirty? I'll send my driver for you.'

Before Kristie could demur the line went dead and she was left wondering what it was that Mrs Mandervell-Smythe was so excited about. But soon work took over and all thoughts of both it and Radford were shut out of her mind.

She loved her work. She loved designing very individual weddings. Each one was a challenge. She needed to get right inside the prospective bride's head to find out what it was she was looking for that would make her wedding a day to remember. Of course she made suggestions of her own, some of which were accepted and some rejected. But Felicity had been full of ideas and opinions herself, knowing exactly what she wanted, and she was able to articulate clearly and precisely. She was a very intelligent young woman and Kristie couldn't help wondering what had put her in a wheelchair.

As soon as Jake was in bed Kristie took a shower and got herself ready. She was hoping that Radford wouldn't be present tonight, whilst knowing that the odds against it were very high. He was taking more interest in his sister's wedding that he would normally have done, Kristie felt sure—and it was her own fault. If she hadn't stupidly given herself away at their first meeting he wouldn't have looked at her twice. She had aroused his curiosity and now was paying for it.

She slipped into a silk dress and jacket in her favourite sky blue—an outfit that she had bought for her cousin's wedding the previous summer, and matching patent high-heeled shoes. She fixed her hair up in a loose tumble of curls and draped long silver earrings in her ears.

'You look fabulous,' breathed Chloe. Her housemate was short and dumpy and always bemoaning the fact that no clothes looked right on her.

'You don't think I've gone over the top?' asked Kristie.

The compliment worried her. She didn't want Radford Smythe thinking that she had dressed up for his benefit.

'You'll knock him dead.' Her friend grinned.

'I'm not going to see Radford, it's his mother,' protested Kristie vehemently.

Chloe shrugged. 'Whatever you say.' But it was clear she didn't believe her. Yesterday, after he'd gone, she'd literally drooled over him. 'What a gorgeous hunk,' she'd said. 'Where did you find him?' And further questions had come thick and fast.

She had been disappointed to find out that Kristie wasn't in the slightest bit interested. 'Just hand him over to me,' she'd said. 'I could do with a real man.'

When the doorbell rang at seven fifteen Chloe eagerly said, 'I'll get it. I want to have another look at Mr Hunk.'

'It won't be him. It will be their chauffeur,' Kristie pointed out. But as it happened it was neither.

'Paul!' she exclaimed as he preceded Chloe into the room. 'What are you doing here?'

'I've had better welcomes,' he complained, but there was a smile on his face. 'I came to ask you out but it looks like I'm too late.'

Paul was tall and lanky with mousy brown hair and hazel eyes and he was the kindest and most genuine man you could ever wish to meet. Jake adored him and he was good with the boy too. Even though he knew Kristie didn't love him in the way he wanted, he still persisted.

'I'm sorry,' she said wistfully.

'Where are you going? Somewhere classy? You look stunning, Kristie.' There was the slightest hint of regret in his voice.

'Dinner at a client's, that's all,' she announced as casually as she could.

The doorbell rang again and Chloe ran eagerly to answer

it. When Kristie heard the deep male voice her heart sank into her shoes. Why Radford? What had happened to the driver?

He stopped dead in his tracks as he walked into the room, looking at Paul with a deep, questioning frown. 'Radford,' spoke Kristie quickly, 'this is Paul Derring, a very dear friend of mine. Paul, meet Radford Smythe. I'm co-ordinating his sister's wedding.'

The two men shook hands, both looking warily at the other. It was Paul who turned away first. 'It's time I went. I'll give you a ring later in the week, Kristie.'

She nodded. 'I'll see you to the door.' She felt Radford's eyes on them both as they left the room, and so it appeared did Paul.

'Am I getting my nose pushed out?' he asked, pausing in the doorway.

'Definitely not,' she asserted. 'I didn't even expect him to come and pick me up. His mother said she was sending her driver.'

'He didn't look pleased to see me. I think he has his eye on you.'

'Nonsense! In any case, he's not my type. Don't worry about him, Paul.' As she spoke she linked her arms around his neck and kissed him with much more meaning than usual. She felt sorry for him because he had turned up to take her out and here she was being picked up by another man.

Taken by surprise, Paul hesitated a moment before returning her kiss with a passion that was rare for him also. Not that he had never wanted to kiss Kate in this way—she was aware of that—but he had always respected her feelings.

When Paul finally left she closed the door and turned around—and discovered Radford watching her, a frown dragging his brows together, his lips unsmiling. 'You amaze me, Kristie Swift. I'd never have guessed you liked the sort of man you can wrap around your little finger. I thought you had more spirit than that. There'll be no excitement in your life with a man like Paul Derring.'

'Who said I want excitement?' she protested swiftly and furiously. She was embarrassed that he had seen her kiss Paul, especially as it had been so out of character, an act of defiance almost. And yet, in a way, perhaps it was a good thing. If Radford thought she and Paul were a permanent item it would keep him off her back. There would be no more dinner invitations, no more wanting to get to know her better.

'You certainly need more than he can offer,' he commented tersely.

'You don't know him,' Kristie tossed back, her eyes flashing green fire.

Thick, well-shaped brows rose. 'I'm a pretty shrewd judge of character.'

'Without even speaking to him?'

'Yes,' he answered confidently. 'If I were him and another guy came into the room who was going to take my girl out to dinner I most definitely wouldn't have walked away and left him. The man's a wimp.'

'How dare you?' Kiristie's fragile hold on her temper was slipping. 'For one thing, it's not you taking me out to dinner, and Paul knew that.' But then an awful thought hit her—one that made her go sick to the bottom of her stomach. She glared accusingly. 'If this is some con-trick, if you think you're going to—'

His smile held no hint of pleasure. 'We *are* dining at my mother's house. Not that I wouldn't have preferred to take you out myself but—'

'Some hope of that,' she snapped, charging past him. But

Radford had other ideas. His arms came out and she was caught in a band of steel. 'Let me show you what it's like to be kissed by a real man.' His voice which had been hard and uncompromising, deepened to a smoky growl.

The feel of that strong-boned body against hers sent an unwanted message to Kristie's brain. This man was dangerous. Not only that but he was filling her senses. It was something she could well do without. Even now he was taking control of her body, her mind and everything else sensual.

When his mouth came down on hers it sent a further assault shuddering through her. One arm remained around the small of her back while his other hand cupped her chin in a grip so hard she wanted to cry out.

And all this happened in the space of a few seconds.

His aftershave was subtle and sensual, teasing her nostrils, adding to the chaos inside her. Every inch of her body responded, while at the same time she knew that it was imperative she escape.

But in the end she didn't have to put up a fight. She was suddenly as free as the air around her—free in the physical sense, but not from the feelings which ran rampant inside her. Feelings this man had managed to arouse in the merest atom of time.

It was deeply worrying and she could see why her sister had been so besotted by him. Her voice was harsh when she spoke. 'That was an appalling thing to do. What would your mother think if she knew you'd assaulted me?'

'Assaulted?' Hot, indignant eyes blazed into hers. 'You call one brief kiss an assault? And actually it lasted a lot less time than the one you gave your boyfriend. Nor can you deny that you found it pleasurable.'

He was right, damn him—the effect of the kiss still lingered, her body felt sizzlingly alive, something it had never done when Paul kissed her. Her eyes sparked and she wiped the back of her hand across her mouth in a deliberately insulting gesture. 'Don't ever do that again.'

'You don't mean that, Kristie. You're angry because you responded to me against your will.' His mouth twitched at the corners and he looked annoyingly relaxed as he leaned back against the doorjamb, his thumbs hooked into his trouser pockets.

'Responded?' she huffed. 'To you? You have to be joking. You're the last man on earth I'd respond to.' Her sister was dead because of this man. She hated him with every breath that she drew. And what she ought to have done was turn that job down the second she found out who she was dealing with.

'Why?'

The direct question caught her by surprise, but not the hard glitter in his eyes. She had expected that. He was a man who didn't take kindly to being spurned. 'Because you think you're God's gift,' she snapped. 'You turn women's heads as inevitably as flowers to the sun, but not this one, I assure you. I have better taste.'

His breath whistled through his teeth and Kristie waited for the onslaught that never came. She could actually see him controlling his temper. 'I think we should go,' he said stiffly.

Kristie knew the time was fast approaching to confront him, yet still she felt a need to know him better. Though how, when all she ever wanted to do was put space between them, she didn't know. This evening was going to be a huge ordeal. It would crucify her being civil to him, but for his mother's and sister's sake she had to do it.

Before they left she popped into the kitchen where a smiling Chloe was lurking out of the way.

'He kissed you,' she breathed, wide eyed as Kristie reapplied her lipstick.

'Paul?'

'No, Mr Hunk. I think he fancies you, and he's a much better catch.'

'Not in my opinion,' declared Kristie strongly, but she didn't want to talk about him. 'You will ring me if Jake wakes and wants me, won't you? I hate leaving him like this, it's—'

'Just go,' ordered Chloe. 'Everything will be all right. Go and enjoy yourself.'

As if she could. And if Chloe knew the whole story she wouldn't be saying this.

The black Mercedes was spacious and sumptuous but as she sank into the soft leather seat Kristie wished it would swallow her up. Radford's sexuality filled the space, drawing her into his web like a spider did a fly. He was a dangerous, threatening male and she needed to be on her guard at all times. It would be so easy to fall for him. That one brief kiss had taught her that. But her brain was sending out warning signals which she'd do well to heed.

'I don't bite,' he snarled as she huddled against the door.

Kristie's eyes flashed. 'I never for one moment thought you did.'

'Then why shrink away from me? My kiss got you rattled, did it? You're afraid I might try it again. Don't worry. You're perfectly safe; I like my women willing.'

His women! Confirming her opinion that he enjoyed playing the field. Why was it that men with money and power thought they could have any girl they wished? Was it a game they played, dumping them when they got tired of them and going on to the next gullible female? It made her mad just thinking about it.

She deigned not to answer him, keeping her eyes on the road ahead and her hands folded tightly in her lap.

'I hope you're not going to keep this up all night,' he rasped. 'My mother will wonder what on earth she's letting herself in for. More than likely she'll cancel the contract. Which, in my opinion, won't be a bad thing. I've had a feeling about you right from the start.'

Kristie's head turned sharply in his direction. 'If you kept your nose out it would be all right. I'm quite capable of liaising with your mother and Felicity. There's no need for you to even be here.'

'My mother thinks there is. Since my father died she finds it difficult to cope. She never had to make decisions; he made them all for her.'

'And you've stepped into his shoes? Is that for her own good? I don't think so. What would happen if there was a catastrophe while you were abroad, let's say? She'd have to cope then. You're doing her no favours.'

'And you're an expert on this, are you?' he charged angrily. 'You're one of the breed of women who think they can do anything a man can do?'

'I know I can,' she retorted.

'Hmph!' he snorted, and then remained in disapproving silence for the rest of the journey.

Radford couldn't understand why Kristie hated him so. He had thought it might be men in general—until she kissed Paul Derring. What she saw in this other man he had no idea. Paul wasn't a man; he was a mouse, meekly skulking away the moment he arrived. It was something he certainly wouldn't have done, he'd have wanted to know exactly what interest this man had in his girlfriend.

Perhaps Paul liked dominant females. Perhaps he liked to be led rather than do the leading. And perhaps this was what Kristie favoured as well. It could be the reason why she was so against him. For once she had met a man who preferred to take charge, and she didn't like it.

He smiled grimly to himself. Kristie Swift was going to prove a challenge. She might not know it yet, but he was determined to win her over. It didn't sit well on his shoulders to be spurned and he had probably made matters worse by kissing her.

But what a kiss. It had been a spur of the moment thing but it had sent his testosterone levels soaring. She had tasted wickedly sweet and her body had been softly feminine and desirable against him, sending a plethora of sensations to his every extremity. He had wanted more; he had wanted to deepen the kiss, he had wanted to touch and stroke and make her his in every way possible.

Considering he had thought her an unbalanced woman to start with, his change of feelings was quite startling. He could hardly believe them himself. Even sitting here, Kristie shying as far away from him as possible, he wanted to reach out and place his hand over hers, assure her that he didn't bite, that it would be all right for her to relax and get to know him properly. Either that or shake her! He had never met anyone so infuriating and for once he was unsure how to deal with a situation.

She looked totally gorgeous in that sky blue suit and if she would only relax it would be a very pleasant evening. He wondered how she would react to the proposal his mother was about to make.

CHAPTER FIVE

'SO WHAT do you think?'

Kristie looked at Mrs Mandervell-Smythe in stunned silence and it was several seconds before she spoke. 'I don't know. You've taken me by surprise. It's very generous of you, but—'

'Radford told me that you work in a corner of your living room. That's no good, my dear, especially as you have a woman and child living with you. How on earth do you cope? It's the perfect solution. Do say yes.'

Mrs Mandervell-Smythe had no idea how impossible the situation was. How could she work in this house with Radford present? The use of a room as an office was a very charitable gesture and it would certainly help matters; it was often difficult to concentrate with Jake running around, even though Chloe did her best to keep him out of the way. But...

'Come, let me show you,' said the older woman decisively.

Kristie paused to glance at Radford as she left the room behind his mother. He had dropped into an armchair, totally relaxed, listening with interest to their conversation. There was an enigmatic smile on his lips now—the sort of smile that told her this was more his doing than his mother's, and she glared at him accusingly.

'Run along,' he said. 'You don't want my mother thinking you're ungrateful, do you?'

'This is your idea, isn't it?' she hissed softly. 'And I

49

don't find it in the least amusing. I think you have a cheek, trying to interfere in my life.'

'How can you work with some damn child around all the time? I merely have your best interests at heart,' he returned, still with that infuriating smile.

'Which I can do without,' she shot back, and to her relief he didn't join her as she hurried to catch up with his mother. They walked through a series of corridors until they reached a room which Kristie judged to be at the west end of the building, well away from their living quarters.

'This was my husband's study,' explained Mrs Mandervell-Smythe as she pushed open the door. 'It's never used these days. Radford has his own office here, of course. In fact, he has his own suite of rooms, but mostly he works from London. Amazingly, this time he's in no hurry to get back. I expect it's because of Felicity's wedding; there's so much to think about and he knows I couldn't do it without him. Nor you, of course, my dear. It's such a relief to have all the work taken off my shoulders.'

Kristie smiled faintly. There was no relief on her part. His mother might be pleased that Radford was staying but she definitely wasn't.

'So what do you think?' asked the older woman as Kristie gazed around the oak-panelled room. 'Could you work here?'

It was a large room with a huge desk and endless shelves. Near one of the two windows which looked out over the garden at the back of the house were two deep leather armchairs. It would be a dream to work here compared to the cramped space she had at home. There was only one drawback.

'It's very generous of you Mrs Mandervell-Smythe—'

'Please, call me Peggy, everyone does.'

Kristie smiled weakly. 'Peggy, then.' Somehow it felt wrong calling Radford's mother by her first name, but she didn't want to argue. 'I don't really feel I can take you up on your offer. It's—'

'Nonsense. You'd be doing me a favour, as a matter of fact. Otherwise we'd be on the phone to each other all of the time. Felicity's a devil for changing her mind, as I think Radford warned you. It simply makes sense.'

Peggy was right and if she was honest with herself it was the offer of a lifetime. Free use of an office! How lucky could she get? But not if Radford was going to be on her back every hour of the day; it would lose all its pleasure. 'Whose idea was it, yours or Radford's?' she asked.

'Mine,' said Peggy instantly. 'As soon as he told me about your working conditions I knew Edward's study would be perfect for you. It's criminal that it never gets used. Please say yes. It won't cost you a penny. You can use this door—' indicating one of the French windows '—and come and go as you please. There's ample parking space round the back here.'

'How about the main gates?'

'I'll give you a remote. There is absolutely no reason why you shouldn't take up my offer. I thought you'd jump at the chance. Why are you hesitating?'

'Perhaps she thinks we'd interfere?'

Kristie turned at the sound of Radford's deep, gravelly voice. Why was *he* butting in? Her green eyes flashed hostility, but before she could say anything his mother spoke.

'Of course we wouldn't; you'd have total privacy, Kristie. You talk to her, Radford. Make her see sense.'

Kristie knew his mother was pressurising her because it helped to have her on the spot, but after the wedding, what then? After the wedding Radford wouldn't be here, she told herself. Nor would he remain here for the whole of the run up to the wedding. It was twelve months away. So why not take advantage of such a liberal offer?

'She knows it makes sense,' he said. 'I think it's me who's the stumbling block.'

His mother frowned. 'What are you talking about?'

'For some reason Kristie Swift has taken a dislike to me.'

Kristie could have spat in Radford's eye. What the hell did he have to say that for? Her gripe with him was private, nothing to do with his parent.

'Nonsense!' his mother said. 'Why would she do that?'

'You'd best ask her.'

'Your son is not why I am hesitating,' Kristie told her firmly. 'In fact—' her mind was suddenly made up '—I'd like to take you up on your offer. It will be a great help. I shall work normal office hours and you'll hardly know I'm here.'

Peggy smiled happily and put her hands together as though praying. 'I'm so pleased, and I'm quite sure you won't regret it. No one will interfere, I can assure you of that. This office will be your private domain. There's a lock on both doors, I'll give you the keys.'

Kristie felt Radford eyeing her but she ignored him, ignored also the skittering of her senses. 'I'll pay for phone calls, of course, and electricity,' she said firmly.

'No, you won't,' insisted the older woman. 'You're doing me the favour by putting the room to some use. I won't hear another word said about it. Move in as soon as you like. Radford, go and find the keys.'

The air cleared the moment he left, but Kristie didn't miss the look he gave her. It was triumph. He had deliberately goaded her into saying yes and she had stupidly fallen for it. And somehow she had the feeling that he wouldn't leave her alone, no matter what his mother said.

She made up her mind there and then that the doors would remain firmly locked.

By the time they got back to the main part of the house Felicity's husband-to-be had arrived and Kristie's fear that she might find herself alone with Radford was quickly dispelled.

Daniel Fielding was perfect for Felicity. Not particularly good looking, but thoughtful and caring and kind and intelligent. And they were both deeply in love. It was there for everyone to see.

Kristie spent some time talking to him but felt Radford's eyes on her, even though he was chatting away to his mother and sister. It was unnerving having him watch her like this; it sent a funny feeling down her spine, and she couldn't help wondering whether his mother noticed his interest in her.

When dinner was announced Radford came across and took her elbow and led her into the dining room. She couldn't ignore the tingles that his touch created and was delighted when she discovered that she was not to be seated next to him. It wasn't long, though, before she discovered that sitting opposite him was just as bad.

'Tell me, Kristie,' said Radford, once their first course had been served, 'what made you decide to become a wedding co-ordinator? You must get so many headaches it can hardly be worthwhile. Have you ever been married yourself? Is that how you realised how much work is involved and that you could save other people a lot of trouble?'

His question aroused everyone's interest but it was to him that she looked. Although he guessed that none of the others could see it, he could tell that she resented him asking such personal questions.

'Actually, no, I've never been married.'

So it wasn't her husband who'd hurt her. It was some other man to whom she'd been attached, someone who was a lot like himself, apparently. He was glad she'd agreed to his mother's offer because now he could work on her. There was an awful lot he wanted to know about Miss Kristie Swift.

'I became a wedding co-ordinator because—well, because I like organising. I'd done various design and management courses over the years and this appealed to me. It's something I enjoy and something I do well.'

'I wonder whether you'll think the same when my darling sister's finished with you.'

'Radford!' hurled Felicity. 'Don't be insulting.'

He grinned. 'You know what you're like, cherub. You don't know your own mind from one minute to the next.'

'Don't believe him,' said Felicity to Kristie. 'He's trying to wind us both up. He's not approved of you from the word go and I don't know why. I think you're perfect for the job and I'm so glad you've agreed to use Daddy's office. I'll be able to come and talk to you and—'

'Darling.' It was Peggy's turn to speak. 'Kristie won't want us interrupting her. We'll still need to go through the usual channels. In fact, Kristie, I shall have a separate telephone line installed. Radford, you'll see to it for me, won't you?'

'Anything you say, Mother.' It was a wry comment and not lost on Kristie. He saw the flicker in her eye, could almost read her mind. There was not much he didn't notice about her. She was thoroughly uncomfortable sitting here with his family and she was wishing herself at home, though how she found any peace there he didn't know. He had thought she would jump at the chance of an office here; was somewhat surprised when it took her so long to make up her mind.

He wasn't stupid enough not to realise that he was the big deciding factor, although she needn't have worried; he wouldn't be here for much longer. Much as he wanted to stay and get to know her better, there were other pressing issues to deal with. His PA had phoned him only that morning with a whole list of queries that needed his personal attention.

Kristie was uncomfortable now beneath his gaze, trying hard to concentrate on eating her seafood medley. There was a pink tinge to her cheeks and an angry flash of green in her eyes. He was pleased his mother had sat her opposite him.

Peggy had despaired of him ever finding the right woman and if she knew exactly which way his thoughts ran she'd do her utmost to throw them together. It would be an all-out blatant attack, one that Kristie would be sure to notice, and one that had frightened off other girls before her.

He sensed Kristie's relief when the meal was finally over. She had toyed with her food, hardly eating a thing, looking at him from beneath her long lashes whenever she had thought he wasn't watching her. She had joined in the conversation, answering easily and interestingly, but when she had been forced to speak to him the shutters had come down.

No one else had seemed to notice, so perhaps he was being too sensitive. Though he doubted it. This woman hated him and he intended to find out why—hopefully when he took her home tonight. Meanwhile, he would take pleasure in looking at her beautiful face and body.

He'd never been out with a redhead before. Not that her hair was exactly red—nearer a light auburn. But the more he saw of her the more he wanted her. There was no denying it. She alerted every male hormone inside him, sent his testosterone levels sky high and his need of her burnt like a furnace. He allowed his foot to touch hers beneath the table and was rewarded by a further blaze of green and another heated flush, revealing that she wasn't exactly immune to him either.

It brought a smile to his lips which in turn sent yet another green flash in his direction. He found it amazing that he enjoyed it when she was angry with him. His whole body ached with a sudden desperate need to bed her. Whether she saw it in his eyes or whether it was her own desperate need to escape, he didn't know, but she suddenly stood up. 'I really ought to be going, Mrs Mandervell— Peggy. I have no wish to outstay my welcome. It's very kind of you to let me use your husband's office. I'll move in after the weekend, if that's all right?'

Peggy beamed. 'It's more than all right. Radford, did you find those keys?'

He'd been hoping his mother wouldn't remember—it would have given him an excuse to see Kristie in her new workplace. Now he fished them out of his pocket and dangled them in front of her nose. 'One set of keys.' And he knew full well that she would keep her door firmly locked. Not against anyone else, just him. It brought a grim expression to his face. What the hell was he doing feeling an interest in this woman? He'd go back to London tomorrow and forget her.

When he stood up too Kristie said quickly, 'Don't put yourself out; I'll call a taxi.'

'No, you won't,' insisted his mother. 'Radford will take you.'

'My mother's given her driver the night off,' Radford explained, his lips compressed at her horrified expression. There was going to be no fun in driving her. All he was going to do was get totally frustrated. Damn the woman. What had he done to upset her, for God's sake?

He determined there and then to drive her straight home and say nothing on the journey. But it didn't work out like that. The very nearness of her heightened and alerted every one of his senses; the scent of her body assailed his nostrils like an aphrodisiac. The thought of dropping her off and walking away was abhorrent.

Kristie didn't shrink against the door this time, so maybe, just maybe, there was faint hope. He wished he knew what dark thoughts ran through her mind, what it was that she held against him. He didn't even know whether it was personal or men in general.

She had said men of his type—but what type was that? As far as he was concerned he was no different from other men. He was successful, yes. He ran a profitable business, but so too did plenty of others. Did she have it in for all of them? She'd seemed to like Daniel Fielding who, in his opinion, wasn't much of a man—even though his beloved sister adored him. He had no great ambitions, he was content to muddle along in his job as a property surveyor. And from what little he'd seen of Paul he was not very much different.

Oddly, Kristie was full of ambition herself. She was doing well with her wedding design company. He could see for himself how dedicated she was and, although he'd said he wanted to check out her credentials, deep down he admired her guts and courage. She would go far.

'Why did you want to leave early?' he asked as he pulled out of the driveway. 'Not that I'm complaining, but I felt you cut the evening short.'

'Did I?' she asked with a frown. 'I hope your mother didn't think that. But it is ten-thirty.'

'And that's your curfew, is it?' he couldn't help asking.

'Not at all,' she answered decisively. 'I was up at five this morning; I'm rather tired.'

He raised a brow as he looked at her. 'I thought you might have been running away from me?' There was an almost full moon slanting into the car, giving her face an icy beauty as she shot him a glance.

'Don't flatter yourself,' she snapped.

'Why? You've been giving a very good impression of disliking me. Though, I have to admit, there have been occasions when your guard has slipped and I've glimpsed beneath the surface a woman of passion.'

He sensed rather than saw her dismay and as he expected she denied it. 'The world would have to end before I felt passionate about you,' she retorted.

'You're denying that when my foot touched yours beneath the table it didn't trigger a response? And don't forget I was watching you closely.' So closely that he had seen a dull flush of desire before it was replaced with blazing fury.

'So what?' she asked with a shrug.

'It's a step in the right direction.'

There was an instant hiss of breath and a flash of those dramatic green eyes. 'Don't flatter yourself. I'm not going to take one single step in your direction.'

He allowed himself a faint smile. 'You'd stand no chance, pretty lady, if I really wanted to assert myself.' Which he did, very much so, despite the fact that he'd told her he liked his women willing. But Kristie Swift was different; she was a challenge. Simply looking at her aroused him to such a degree that he knew he wouldn't be content until he had bedded her. And it wasn't simply that. She was interesting in other ways. She was well-educated, intelligent, charming, funny—yes, funny. He had seen her making Daniel and Felicity laugh, and it had peeved him that he couldn't share. She would make a good friend.

Who was he kidding? It was more than friendship he wanted. He wanted her body. Even now, when she was openly rejecting him, his hot male blood surged through veins and arteries with a force that left him breathless.

'I think you're overestimating yourself, Mr Smythe,' she tossed back. 'You can fling anything you like at me and I'll resist it.'

She was feisty, he'd give her that, but if anything it increased his hunger. 'Is that a challenge?'

Frosty eyes glared. 'Actually, no. I expect you to behave like a gentleman.'

'You think I can keep away from someone as excitingly sexy as yourself?' She was asking the impossible.

'Is that how you see me?' she shot back. 'A sex object? Why am I not surprised? You were clearly brought up with a silver spoon in your mouth. Whatever you asked for you were given. And it's my guess it's the same with the opposite sex. You give a smile and lift a finger and the object of your attention comes running. Well, tough luck in my case because this girl's not interested.'

Strong words! He needed to convince her that she was wrong, that he wasn't like that, that he'd worked his way to the top on his own merits. But he knew that she'd flatly refuse to believe him if he told her now. Getting to know her, letting her find out about him, needed to be a gradual process. The trouble was he knew he wouldn't be very big on patience where Kristie Swift was concerned. He was too hungry for her.

'I see you don't deny it,' she tossed scathingly.

'Would you believe me if I did?'

'Of course not.'

'So there's no point. What I think we should do is get to know each other slowly. In that way you'll find out for yourself that I'm not the ogre you seem to think.' He changed down the gears as they approached a set of traffic lights, glancing at her questioningly as he stopped.

'I actually want nothing further to do with you,' she declared. 'I'll be glad when you go back to London.'

Her flat statement not only disappointed him, it angered him. Her attitude towards him was unwarranted. 'How the hell can you talk like that when you don't know me?'

'I don't want to know you,' she riposted.

His breath whistled through his teeth. 'Well, bad luck, because you're going to see an awful lot of me while you're working for my mother.' Now, why had he said that when it was his intention to go back to London? Indeed, he must go. But he would be back, he knew that. He wasn't going to let it end here.

'In that case,' she retorted, 'I won't take up your mother's offer. I saw it as somewhere peaceful I could work, not a hell-hole to be tormented by you. And I'll let you tell her the reason why.'

Radford's lips were grim as he shot away from the traffic lights. He was handling this whole thing badly, which was unlike him. He was renowned for his tact and diplomacy. But not, it appeared, where this young woman was concerned. She rubbed him up the wrong way at every turn.

'There's no need for you to upset my mother,' he said quietly.

'So you'll keep out of my way?'

He couldn't promise that. He wanted to see more of her, a lot more. 'I'm returning to London tomorrow.'

Her relief was palpable and he had no intention of ruining things by admitting that he would be returning. Let her think that he'd gone for a long time.

When they reached Kristie's house he killed the engine and got out of the car.

'You don't have to see me in,' she said hastily.

'Oh, but I do, it's the gentlemanly thing.' He waited for a backlash; was surprised when there was none.

She simply inserted her key fiercely into the lock and opened the door, turning only briefly to say, 'Thank you for the lift.' And then it was shut in his face.

CHAPTER SIX

KRISTIE drove to her new office on Monday morning filled with more than a little trepidation. She had been uneasy the whole weekend, wondering whether she was making a huge mistake, and once or twice had even lifted the phone, prepared to call the whole thing off.

But offers like this came once in a lifetime and she would be a fool to turn it down. Radford was returning to London—so why was she worrying? Perhaps because she didn't believe him.

She pressed her remote control as she approached the immense iron gates. They glided slowly open and she drove her car as near as she could to the long study windows. The idea was that if she could sneak in this way, instead of going through the house, then there was less chance of Radford, if he was still here, discovering her presence.

It was a total shock to see a whole host of new equipment—computer, laser printer, scanner, copier—everything she could possibly need, even a laptop. Stationery, pens, pencils, a drawing board. It was unbelievable, and she felt distinctly uncomfortable. How could they spend all this money on her on top of not wanting any rent? It would tie her to them for ever more. She couldn't do it.

She was on the verge of leaving when a tap came on the door. 'Kristie, it's Peggy.'

With a wry grimace she turned the key.

'What do you think?' asked the older woman, a smile a mile wide on her face. 'I asked Radford to install everything he thought you'd need, but if he's forgotten anything then—'

'Peggy, I can't. It's too much,' protested Kristie.

'Nonsense! It's giving me so much pleasure. Don't spoil it.'

'But it must have cost an awful lot of money.'

'So what? I can afford it. I have little to spend my money on these days. I don't go on holiday any more, I don't enjoy it without Edward, and I have wardrobes full of clothes. It makes me feel good to do this for you. I know you might find this strange, Kristie, but I feel an affinity with you. I feel as though we could be good friends.'

Kristie liked Peggy too; she was a warm and caring woman and although there was a huge age gap it didn't feel like it. But as for being friends, with Radford on the horizon, it was not a good prospect. What would Peggy say, she wondered, if she found out how he had treated her sister, how he had summarily ended their affair when he'd tired of her? Whose side would she take? It was a delicate situation and she ought to have thought this through before accepting her offer.

'It's kind of you to say that, Peggy,' she said sincerely, 'since we hardly know each other. You're being far too kind.'

'I took to you the instant I met you. You're the sort of girl I'd like Radford to marry. Not that I think he ever will get married. He's thirty eight, for goodness' sake, and not a sign of a wife on the horizon. He's happy enough though, running the business. He likes London, he loves the hustle and bustle of a big city. His apartment overlooks the Thames, so he has some breathing space. I couldn't see him ever settling down here.'

Kristie's relief was enormous. 'Did he live here as a child?'

'Oh, yes, this house has been in my husband's family for generations. He loved the open spaces then. He was a proper outdoor boy. Before Felicity's accident they were inseparable.'

'So what happened to your daughter?' It was a question Kristie had longed to ask.

Peggy's face grew sad for a moment. 'She fell off her horse. A proper daredevil she was. She tried to take a hedge far too high. He reared, she fell off, landed on her back and broke her spine. She was only eleven at the time. But she's brave, she never lets it get her down.'

'I can see that,' said Kristie. 'She's remarkably cheerful. I admire her deeply.'

'And now she's found herself a wonderful man who'll look after her for the rest of her life.'

'He's one in a million,' agreed Kristie, 'and I'm honoured to be arranging their wedding.'

'So you don't feel too badly of me for equipping your office? I do want you to be settled here.'

'You're more than generous, Peggy, but I would still feel better if you'd let me pay some rent.'

'You don't want to feel a charity case, is that it?' asked the other woman with an understanding smile. 'Very well, we'll sort something out. Now, tell me, is there anything else that you need? Molly will bring you morning coffee and afternoon tea, and I'd really appreciate it if you'd take lunch with me.'

But Kristie shook her head. 'Thank you, but I'm either out or too busy for lunch. I usually grab a sandwich on the run. Has Radford gone back to London?'

Peggy's attention was successfully diverted. 'Yes, he went last night, much to my surprise. As soon as he got back he packed his bags and left. Said he had some urgent business first thing this morning. I don't suppose I'll see him again for ages.'

Relief washed over Kristie. Now she could get on with her work without having to worry that she might be disturbed by the one man in the world who challenged her senses against her will. He was someone she had never wished to meet. If the event happened, then she had vowed to give him a piece of her mind he would never forget. So why hadn't she? Why had she allowed herself to be attracted to him? Was this how it had happened with Tarah? Had her sister been drawn to him against her will as well?

When Paul found out that she had moved office he wasn't pleased. 'I distrusted that guy right from the moment I met him. It was his idea, wasn't it? He's after you, Kristie, can't you see that?'

He had called to see her that same evening and Kristie had been full of enthusiasm about her new office. 'You're wrong,' she told him now. 'It was Radford's mother who suggested it. He's not there any more. He's gone back to London.'

Paul looked only slightly mollified. 'I still think it's the wrong thing to do. I thought you were happy working from home?'

'I was but Peggy was very insistent, and it makes sense. Jake often interrupts me at all the wrong times. I shall get my work done a lot more quickly.'

'Can you afford it, though? You always said working from home made financial sense.'

She didn't want to admit that she'd been offered it for nothing, even though Peggy was now going to come up with a figure, which she suspected would be nominal anyway, so she shrugged. 'My business is doing OK. It's time I moved on.'

'Does that mean it will be a nine to five job now and you'll have more time for me?' he asked hopefully.

'I guess so,' she admitted. And she knew Jake would love having Paul around more.

In fact, Paul visited her every evening that week, coming early so that he could play with Jake, and then either taking her out for a meal or eating in with her. If it hadn't been for thoughts of Radford lurking in the back of her mind, Kristie would have relaxed and enjoyed herself. She'd always felt comfortable in Paul's company; they never argued, they simply rubbed along easily together.

It was on the second Monday in her new office that Kristie's peace was disturbed. Peggy had taken to visiting her for a few minutes each morning and safe in the knowledge that Radford was in London, she'd got into the habit of leaving the door unlocked. But this morning the tap was louder than normal, and she didn't even have time to call out before the door was pushed roughly open.

She knew before she even saw him who it was. His mother always waited to be invited, but not this man. He strode confidently into the room, a black polo shirt and black trousers making him seem more threatening than normal. 'What are you doing here?' she asked coldly.

He smiled, a grim smile that set her teeth on edge. 'Polite as usual I see.'

'You're supposed to be in London.'

'My mother needed me.'

'Why, what's wrong?' Peggy had been all right when she left on Friday.

'She's not ill, don't worry. A few discussions about the wedding. I warned you Flick would change her mind.'

'And she needed to discuss them with you, not me?' asked Kristie sharply.

'She wanted to talk them over *before* she spoke to you. Have you had a good weekend?'

'I'm sure my private life's very low on your list of priorities,' she tossed scathingly. 'Why are you here? To tell me about the changes, or to torment me?'

'Is that what I do?' His lips quirked, brows rose. 'Why is that, I wonder?'

Kristie heaved an impatient sigh. 'Will you tell me why you're here and then go—please.' If this was going to happen on a regular basis then she really had made a big mistake. Last week had been heaven, this week looked like being a nightmare.

'I merely popped in to ask whether you'd let me take you out to dinner this evening?'

'You're not going back to London?'

'In good time,' he answered with a devilish smile. 'What's your answer?'

'I think you know,' she told him shortly.

He crossed the room and sank down into one of the leather armchairs, looking for all the world as though he'd come to stay. 'I've spent this last week thinking about you,' he told her. 'Wondering why you hate me so much. Oh, I know what you've said but it doesn't ring true. So—here I am and here I intend to stay.'

Kristie's heart clocked along at a disturbing rate. She would have preferred to wait until after the wedding before there was any altercation between them. She didn't want to upset his mother. But could she wait? Not if he was going to pester her like this, that was a fact. He would goad her and goad her until she blurted it out.

But not, she thought suddenly, if she pretended to have a change of heart. Not if she apparently warmed towards him. Could she do that? It was a case of having to if she didn't want to upset Peggy. They had become very close this past week. Peggy had confided all sorts of things in her, and she couldn't bear the thought of doing anything to spoil her pleasure in Felicity's wedding.

'It looks like I have no choice,' she said as evenly as she could.

His smile was triumphant. 'I'll prove to you that I'm not the big bad wolf you think I am.'

'We'll see,' she said quietly. 'Now, if you wouldn't mind, I do have a lot of work to get through.'

'What time are you likely to finish here?' he asked, pushing himself to his feet and coming to stand directly in front of her.

Kristie could smell the woody scent of his aftershave and it sent a prickle of awareness through her senses. This was going to be the most dangerous thing she had ever done. 'Usually around five, but I shall naturally need to go home and get changed.'

'I'll pick you up at your house, then,' he said. 'Shall we say about seven-thirty?'

She nodded.

'Good. I look forward to it.'

But she didn't. She was falling well and truly into his trap. It would be difficult, if not impossible, not to respond to his overt sexuality—and that was the last thing she wanted. Hopefully, though, he wouldn't be here very often. She could cope with the odd few days now and then.

Concentration was impossible and she was glad when she received a phone call that necessitated her going to see one of her other clients. It was six-thirty before she finally got home and it was a mad rush then to bathe Jake and get him ready for bed. She wouldn't have missed Jake's bath time for the world. Sometimes she felt guilty for leaving him with Chloe, and she always tried to make up for it with plenty of hugs and kisses and reassurances of love.

He was asleep by the time Radford came and she was able to greet him calmly and walk out to his car without showing the turmoil that knotted her stomach. All she had to do was have a good time and ignore all the other signs.

But that was easier said than done. It started in the car—just the feel of him next to her was enough. He managed somehow to haunt her senses without even looking at her, without saying a word. It was a strange sensation. She'd never met a man before who aroused her simply by being there.

And in the restaurant, a secluded, cosy little place in the country—she'd not even known that it existed even though it was only a few miles from her home—the sensations continued. Radford didn't say a word out of place. He was the perfect gentleman and yet, sitting opposite him, being forced to look at him, to breathe in the very essence of him, she became so stimulated that she half-expected him to see it, to comment on it.

Of course he couldn't know how she was feeling deep down inside. No, not deep down—everywhere, even the surface of her skin sizzled. She couldn't understand how she could react like this to a man she had hated for the last five years. It didn't make sense. How could she look at him and get an immediate sexual response? It made nonsense of all the harsh thoughts she had harboured against him.

During the meal they talked mainly about his sister's wedding; it was a safe topic and she was happy to discuss it. 'Your mother told me how Felicity came to be in a wheelchair,' she said softly.

Radford pursed his lips and nodded slowly, his eyes shadowing. 'I feel partly to blame,' he said, putting down his knife and fork. 'I was with her at the time and should have tried to stop her. She was so headstrong; a mind of her own, even at that age. The memory of that accident, when she lay there so pale and lifeless, will remain with me for ever.'

This was a side of Radford that Kristie hadn't seen. A side that made him more human and vulnerable. A very different image from the one she had always carried in her mind. Not that it made her think any differently about him, but she could see now why he was always so attentive to his sister's needs. It was his way of trying to make up.

'How did she take it when she learned that she would never walk again?'

Radford winced. 'Very badly. She was angry with everyone for a long time. Temper tantrums became the norm. My mother was at her wits' end.'

'I don't think I'd be happy either,' agreed Kristie. In fact she couldn't think of anything worse.

'But gradually she accepted the inevitable and became her usual cheery, sunny self. I'm so glad she met Daniel. He's perfect for her.' Radford picked up his cutlery and resumed his meal.

They had both ordered fish as their main course, Radford the trout and Kristie poached salmon with a herb crumb topping, which she found truly delicious. 'I've never organised a wedding for anyone in a wheelchair before. It's certainly opened my eyes.'

'From what I hear you're doing a very good job,' he said, his grey eyes warm and kind. 'I take back what I said in the beginning about you not being up to it.'

'Apology accepted,' she said with a demure smile. Feelings were still churning inside her but they had settled down somewhat and to her amazement she found that she was enjoying herself. She was actually beginning to relax. Something she had never expected to do in Radford's company.

Perhaps it was because he was being the perfect gentleman. No advances, no cross words either, simply good conversation. The only hiccup was when he said, 'Tell me about yourself. Do you realise I know nothing about you.'

She tried to turn it into a joke. 'A woman of mystery, that's me.'

He sat back in his seat, a smile playing on his lips as he looked at her. 'It's up to me to guess, is that what you're saying?'

'Not at all. My relationship with your family is purely professional. My private—life is just that, private.' It would be so easy to give too much away and the time still wasn't right.

He cocked his head to one side and looked at her long and hard. 'I was hoping that tonight you might let your hair down and enjoy yourself.'

'I am,' she admitted. 'Very much so, actually.'

'And it surprises you?'

'Well, yes.'

'So you're beginning to realise that I'm not the ogre you think I am?' And all the time his smile was very much in evidence. Not a voracious smile, a warm friendly one that made her feel good inside. In fact her whole body was glowing with pleasure, something she had never expected where this man was concerned.

She picked up her wine glass and took a sip, and for some reason she couldn't take her eyes away from his. That one sip became two, and then another, and before she knew it she had finished the whole glass.

All evening Radford had been attentive to her every need and he did not fail her now. Rather than let the wine waiter do his duty he broke their eye contact to refill it himself, but the action brought his hand dangerously close to hers where she had left it holding the glass.

Kristie half-expected him to touch her, but he didn't. The

smile remained though, and it was not until their plates were taken away and dessert menus placed in front of them that their attention was diverted from each other. They both chose the raspberry pavlova.

'We have a lot more in common than you think,' quipped Radford. 'Let me see, you like your coffee black with just a little sugar?'

She nodded.

'So do I. How about tea? Do you like tea?'

'Not much.'

'Nor me. We're two of a kind, wouldn't you say?'

'I wouldn't go that far,' she said, but she couldn't help smiling.

All in all it was a fun evening, no hint of tension, simply two people having a good time. Even when she caught Radford looking at her with a curious smile, the sort of smile that told her he knew about the emotions churning her stomach, it didn't worry her. So long as he didn't mention them then all would be well.

On the return journey, though, in the close confines of his car, she couldn't ignore them any longer. He'd got through to her whether she wanted him to or not and she was glad when they got home. It was time now to free herself of his presence.

He accompanied her to her front door and this time she didn't feel that she could slam it in his face. 'Would you like to come in for another coffee?' she asked reluctantly, hoping against hope that he would refuse. He'd had one glass of wine and two cups of coffee in the restaurant.

'How about your ten-thirty curfew?' he asked with a straight face.

'I think I could stretch it,' she said.

'Then I'd be delighted to accept your offer.'

But the moment she opened the door Jake came racing along the hall, tears streaming down his little face. 'Mummy, Mummy,' he called. 'I've been waiting for you.' Kristie heard Radford's surprised intake of breath.

CHAPTER SEVEN

'JAKE, darling, what's wrong?' Kristie bent down to fold him in her arms, brushing his tears away with a gentle finger.

'My tummy hurts.'

'Where's Chloe? Has she given you anything for it?'

He shook his head and at that moment Chloe came into the hallway. 'He's not long woken, poor little mite. All he wanted was his mummy.'

'I think I'd better go.' Radford's hard voice broke into their conversation. 'I'll see you tomorrow, Kristie.'

She didn't even look round as he left. All Kristie was interested in was her son's well-being.

Jake was Kristie's son! Radford scowled as he returned to his car. Her son! How had that happened? Stupid! He knew how it had happened. But why hadn't she told him? Why had she let him believe that he belonged to Chloe? Or had she? Had he simply assumed?

And who the devil was the father? Surely not Paul? No, he'd have moved in if that was the case. Some other man she'd ensnared as surely as she was ensnaring him.

Damn! Just when he'd thought he'd found the perfect woman. He pulled his thoughts up short. Perfect? Kristie? When she hadn't hidden her dislike of him? What was he thinking? Yes, they'd had an enjoyable evening—more than enjoyable, in fact. It had taken every ounce of his willpower not to make a move on her. But to call her perfect? Not by a long chalk.

One thing was clear, though. Whoever it was who had done this to her was the one who had made her wary of men. More than wary, in fact—downright hostile towards them. Only Paul seemed to be in favour. And even he hadn't managed to work his way into her home. This woman had a real problem. He might as well forget her.

He wished now that he hadn't let his mother persuade Kristie to make her office with them. The less he saw of her the better. London, here I come, he decided. And nothing except an emergency will bring me back to Warwickshire.

But it didn't work out. The following morning his mother had an appointment with her doctor for her annual check, and Felicity wanted him to help with something to do with her wedding.

'Isn't that what you're employing that damn woman for?' he barked.

'My, my, who's upset you?' she asked with a big grin. 'Didn't your evening go as planned?'

His frown was sharp. 'What do you know about it?'

'There's not much goes on in this house that I don't know about,' she tossed back. 'Want to tell me?'

'There's nothing to tell,' he snarled. 'What is it you wanted to discuss?'

It was mid morning before they finished and by then he was so aware of Kristie in the house that he knew he had to go and see her. He'd observed her car pull up on the drive, seen her get out wearing a smart ivory trouser suit and matching, ridiculously high-heeled shoes. He'd watched the sway of her hips as she walked to the French windows. His testosterone had pumped—violently. Lord, that woman was a menace. She might be a deceptive little witch, but she certainly had what it took to arouse every one of his base instincts.

He rapped sharply on her door and turned the handle. Complete resistance. He cursed silently beneath his breath. He'd wanted to walk in, not give her the chance to refuse to see him, though why he thought she might do that he wasn't sure. They'd had a very pleasant time last night, he'd done or said nothing to upset her, so she had no reason to lock him out. Except that she probably knew he'd want to know why she hadn't told him about her son. And she clearly didn't want to talk.

'Open the door, Kristie,' he said loudly.

No response.

'Dammit, open the door.'

'I'm busy,' came the faint reply. She had a beautiful melodious voice which brushed across his nerve-endings and caused the hairs on his body to stand to attention. He'd noticed from the beginning how lovely her voice was, how well she spoke. There was nothing harsh about her at all— even when she was angry.

Radford shook his head trying to banish these thoughts. They were wrong. He wanted nothing to do with this— gorgeous creature. These last words slipped unbidden into his mind and he tried to dash them away. She was deceitful, a liar, she hated him. How could she be gorgeous? Turn around and run, he told himself firmly. But his hand lifted seemingly of its own volition and knocked on the door again.

He heard the sound of movement and then the key turned and the door swung wide. Kristie had taken off the jacket to her suit revealing a silky sleeveless top, also in ivory, which faithfully followed the line of her curves. His eyes were inevitably drawn to her breasts, high and pert and beautiful. He couldn't help himself. Desire throbbed painfully through him, making him angry with both himself and her.

'Why did you lock me out?' he snarled.

'You think that's what I did? Why would I do that?' she asked, her finely shaped eyebrows rising delicately.

'You tell me.'

'I think you have a complex.'

Radford snorted savagely. 'Why didn't you tell me the boy was yours?' Lord, he hadn't meant to blurt it out like that. It was none of his business. What was she doing to him?

Kristie closed the door and returning to her desk sat down. Very quietly she said, 'I wasn't aware that I had to tell you anything.'

'We sat last night and talked, or at least I talked. You refused even then to tell me anything about yourself. What's the big secret?'

'There is none,' she answered calmly. 'I'm a very private person. I don't discuss my affairs with all and sundry.'

'And that's who I am, Mr All and Sundry?' he barked, really beginning to lose his temper now, especially as she was being so reasonable, when what he wanted was a blazing row. He needed to clear the air. 'I thought I was beginning to mean a little more to you than that.'

'Then you're kidding yourself,' she answered. 'I have a business arrangement with your mother, and that's as close as you and I are going to get.'

'How old's the boy?'

'You mean Jake?' she asked, her calmness beginning to desert her. There was a tartness to her voice now.

'Yes, I mean Jake.'

'Five.'

'And who's Chloe?' he demanded.

'His babysitter, his nanny, my home help, whatever you like to call her.'

'Where's the child's father?'

She paused a moment, eyeing him coldly, appearing to consider whether to tell him. Her mind made up, she lifted her chin determinedly. 'It's no business of yours.'

Of course it wasn't, but, hell, he wanted to know. 'He's the one who did the hatchet job on you?'

'Exactly,' she retorted, her cheeks flushing now. 'He's a swine of the highest order.'

'And well out of your life?'

There was a slight hesitation. 'I'd like him to be.'

Radford frowned. 'He's still hanging around?'

'I met him recently.'

'I hope you told him where to get off.' If he ever bumped into the guy who'd given her such a complex he'd take great delight in dealing with him himself.

'He doesn't take no for an answer easily.'

'Perhaps you need police protection?' He couldn't bear the thought of her being intimidated. 'Can I help?'

She smiled then, a slow, sad smile. 'I don't think it will come to that. And I can handle myself, thank you very much.'

It was with reluctance that he let the matter drop. 'How's your son now? Is his tummy better?'

'He's fine,' answered Kristie. 'He'd overindulged on jelly and ice cream. Thank you for asking, but I'm sure you're not really interested.'

He didn't like children, Tarah had told her that. Her sister had not had an inkling that he was going to end their relationship and had reached the conclusion that it was because she'd talked about marriage and family. So why was he asking about Jake now?

'Dammit, Kristie. How can you say that?' he demanded, striding over to her desk.

'Easily,' she replied, calmly looking up at him, hoping

he couldn't see her inner turmoil. 'You don't strike me as a man who likes children.' Not only because Tarah had told her but because he'd called Jake a 'damn child' the first time he'd ever seen him. 'How can you work with some damn child around all the time?' he'd asked.

'And how have I given that impression?' he rasped harshly. He splayed his hands on the desk and towered menacingly above her. Careful, Kristie warned, you're going to give yourself away. The idea had dawned on her last night that she could get her revenge on Radford for causing the death of her sister, even though indirectly, by keeping secret the fact that Jake was his son. How cruel was that? The very thought delighted her. It wasn't normally in her nature to behave like this but Radford Mandervell-Smythe had done one very bad thing, and for that she could never forgive him.

'Never mind about how,' she retorted.

He shook his head and pushed away from her. 'You're a very strange woman to understand. You're more complex than I first thought.'

'And that troubles you, does it?' she scorned. She wanted him to be troubled, deeply troubled, like she'd been in the days after her sister's death. It had been the biggest upheaval of her life. Losing her beloved Tarah and being landed with a new baby had almost threatened her sanity.

She'd toyed with the idea of finding Radford and dumping the child on his doorstep—only the fact that she knew Tarah wouldn't like it had stopped her. But in truth Jake was his responsibility, and in some small measure using this office rent-free—because his mother had still not come up with any figure—was what she deserved. Except, of course, that it was his mother footing the bill and not Radford. Although, she argued with herself, as it was still a family business he was indirectly paying.

'I'd like to get to know you better.' He looked away as he spoke as though he was already regretting the words.

'I don't think that would be a very good idea,' she retorted. 'We have nothing in common.' Except a dear little boy named Jake.

A horrifying thought struck her. If Radford ever did find out that Jake was his then he would do his utmost to take him from her, even though she had officially adopted him. Another very good reason why she must never tell him. She had grown to love Jake as though he was her own and couldn't bear the thought of him being taken away from her.

'You intrigue me,' he said.

'And that's a good enough reason why I should see more of you?' she questioned coldly. 'I don't think so. In fact, I'd like it if you went now and never came back.'

'You didn't enjoy yourself last night?'

Kristie couldn't lie. 'Actually, yes I did, much to my surprise.'

'But you wouldn't care to repeat it?'

'I see no point.'

His breath hissed out through his teeth. 'Actually I was going back to London today, but I think I might hang around for a few days. I enjoy a challenge.'

Kristie was horrified. 'What do you mean, a challenge?' She knew very well what he meant but she needed to hear it put into words.

'I want to prove to you,' he announced loftily, 'that all men are not the same.'

'And you think you could do that?' she demanded with a toss of her head and a flash of her electric green eyes.

An odd little smile came to his lips—a confident smile that only served to infuriate her further. 'I'd like to give it a try.'

'You'd be wasting your time,' she proclaimed strongly.

'But you're not saying that I cannot?'

What would be the point? Radford was the sort of guy who could railroad anybody into anything. If he was really determined she wouldn't have a leg to stand on. 'Would that stop you?'

His smile now was genuine. 'You're getting to know me.'

Worse luck! This was a man she had never wanted to meet and she had the awful feeling that she was going to dig herself into a hole far deeper than she was prepared to go. Where are your guts, girl? she asked herself. This isn't what you want, so say so, for goodness' sake.

She couldn't. There was one tiny part of her that was attracted to this man. And that tiny part was taking over. It wanted to see more of him. It wanted to enjoy the buzz of excitement she felt when he was near. It wanted to taste his kisses. It wanted to reach out and touch him, to feel that hard, finely honed body against hers.

The very thought sent her mouth dry and she touched her tongue to her lips and saw a flash in Radford's eyes and the way he drew in a swift breath. She prayed he hadn't read her mind or it would all be over. Any protests would be in vain.

'We'll have lunch together,' he announced.

His audacity shouldn't have surprised her but it did. He really did think that he could snap his fingers and she would jump. Probably most girls did, but not this one. Oh, no. She looked at her watch. 'That's impossible. I have an appointment at two.' Liar! She'd planned to spend all day here.

'Then we'll have an early lunch.'

Kristie shook her head vehemently. 'I don't have time for proper lunches. I have sandwiches in my bag.'

'Then I'll have sandwiches too and join you.'

He made it sound so simple and yet simple their relationship could never be. But there was no stopping him, she knew that, and so she shrugged. 'If that's what you want, but I'm warning you, it will be a short lunch. I'm very busy.'

Not until he had gone could she breathe easy again and she found it hellishly difficult to concentrate. It seemed like only minutes before he was back—with a bottle of wine, two glasses, a plate of sandwiches and a bowl of salad. 'We'll share,' he announced confidently.

'You do realise I'm driving afterwards?' flashed Kristie. 'I can't possibly drink wine.'

'It's non alcoholic,' he told her with a smile. 'A fruity drink, that's all. But it looks like the real thing. Shall we take it out on the lawn?'

Kristie knew she was lost. There was no point in demurring. The lawn overlooked the swimming pool which she had looked at several times with great longing but had never dared ask whether she could use it

He unrolled a blanket and she sat down and opened her lunch box but didn't feel like eating. Radford poured the wine and she sipped that instead. It was surprisingly refreshing, beautifully chilled and slightly sparkling. It was peaceful here and as she looked around she spotted a hoist at the far end. 'Does your sister use this pool for therapeutic purposes?' she asked.

Radford nodded. 'Most days—except in the winter, of course. I did want to have one put in the house but my mother wouldn't let me.'

'Will Felicity still live here when she's married?' She was happy with these safe topics. Not happy with the way her body was behaving, but he was not to know that.

'Yes. We have everything here for her convenience. A

suite of rooms has been prepared for them so they'll have their independence. She's so excited.'

'It's going to be a beautiful wedding.'

'I have only your word for that.'

'Believe me, I won't let you down. It will be a day to remember.' That was what she called her business—A Day to Remember. And at every single wedding she had organised the brides had said afterwards that it definitely had been a memorable day. She tried to make each one unique and Felicity's was going to be the grandest of them all.

'Do you think you'll ever get married yourself? Or will your hatred of men last a lifetime?'

Kristie had been looking at the sunlight glinting on the water. Now she turned and met Radford's enquiring eyes. 'I don't hate all men,' she told him sharply. His eyes were narrowed against the sun, silvery and penetrating, and tiny shivers of excitement began to dance through her veins.

'Oh, I forgot, there's Paul, isn't there?' he drawled. 'Tell me, does Paul set you on fire the way I do?'

The audacity of the man! He'd said it so calmly, as though it was a perfectly ordinary question. How could he know? Surely she hadn't given herself away? 'In your dreams,' she said with a faint laugh, hoping to make a joke of it.

'You can't deny it. I've seen that give-away pulse in your throat. I've actually felt the heat of your skin. I bet it's hot now.'

He leaned forward and touched her arm, letting his fingers slide right up to her shoulder and then slowly across to her throat, where his thumb rested on the pulse in question. And there was precious little she could do about it.

She didn't say a word. She couldn't; she was totally hypnotised by what he was doing. At the same time she steeled herself not to respond because, goodness, she wanted to.

She wanted to lay her hand over his, she wanted to touch him too, feel the heat of *his* body. Oh, lord! This was all wrong. This was insanity. This wasn't in the plan of things at all.

She dashed his arm away angrily. 'What the hell are you playing at?'

He grinned, a wicked, white, predatory smile. 'You're beautiful when you're angry. Those delicate green eyes of yours darken and flash fire and your face becomes animated. It makes me want to kiss you.' Even as he spoke he leaned towards her and hooked a hand behind her head so that there was no escape, then his mouth came down on hers.

CHAPTER EIGHT

KRISTIE knew that she would look back on this moment and ask herself why she hadn't jerked away from Radford, but for some reason she remained motionless. She accepted his kiss. It was a fatal thing to do, it gave entirely the wrong impression. She began to struggle, but not before she had felt the full impact of a kiss so dangerous that the memory would be with her for all time.

It was an assault on her senses. Tingles ran from the tips of her toes and fingers and congregated in her stomach. Blood pumped through her veins at an alarming speed. It rushed through her head and she could hear the hammer throb of her heart and pulses. The intoxicating maleness of him filled her nostrils and she could taste the sweetness of the wine on his lips.

'That wasn't so bad, was it?' he asked, letting her go when she had thought he would persist. 'In fact, I gained the distinct impression that you found it pleasurable. It was your conscience that made you put a stop to it. I oughtn't to be kissing this man, you told yourself, it goes against my principles.'

He was so right, but she wasn't going to admit that. She picked up her wine glass and tossed back the remains. 'You're far wide of the mark.'

'Then why didn't you stop me from the beginning?' he asked. 'Come on, admit it, you were as curious as I. And reality was greater than the dream, wouldn't you say?'

Kristie tossed her head, her eyes flashing angrily. 'Since

I've never dreamt about kissing you I cannot answer that question.'

'What a little liar you are,' he said with a knowing smile. 'But I'll forgive you—for the moment. Eat your sand-wiches.'

How could she eat when her body was on fire? 'I'm not hungry,' she said and glanced at her watch. 'I really should be going.'

'Running away won't solve anything.'

'I'm not running away.'

'So why do you want to leave so suddenly? We've been here less than ten minutes.'

'I think you know why,' she snapped. 'I didn't come out here to be mauled by a beast like you.'

Her harsh words, said in the heat of the moment and unforgivably rude, had a dramatic effect on him. His smile faded, nostrils flared, and she had the feeling that if she'd been a man he would have punched her.

'Dammit woman, no one speaks to me like that. I would never *maul* someone, as you so crudely put it. You're scared of your own feelings; that's the trouble. They're making a mockery of your *pretension* of hating men. It's gone on so long that you haven't even realised that your values have changed.' He got up then and glared down at her. 'Do you know what? I pity you. You're going to lead an awfully lonely life.'

Kristie scrambled to her feet. 'You know nothing,' she declared heatedly.

'I know you're one very mixed up lady.'

Maybe she was. And he was the one who had done it. She grabbed her sandwich box and with a further heated glare in his direction headed back to her office. She spent an hour there fuming. It was the last straw when she went out to her car and found it wouldn't start.

She lifted the bonnet and looked in vain beneath it. She didn't know anything about engines but maybe, just maybe, something might jump out at her. A loose lead, perhaps? Anything, please, she prayed. I need to get away from here.

She heard Radford's footsteps crunching on the gravel. 'Having trouble?' And she groaned inwardly, even though she knew that she needed his help. He slid behind the wheel and turned the key. The engine gave a grunt and a groan but that was all. Her car was fifteen years old and had only recently begun to give her trouble. But why now of all times?

'Mmm,' he said, coming to stand beside her. 'It sounds as though it's your starter motor. I'll call someone out and meantime I think I'd better run you to your destination.'

'I'm going home,' she declared stiffly. 'My appointment's been cancelled. But I don't wish to put you to any trouble. I'll call a taxi.' She fished her mobile out of her bag but Radford would hear none of it.

'Nonsense. I have nothing planned for this afternoon. It will be my pleasure.'

Grim pleasure by the look of it. He still wore a tight expression and he was careful to keep his distance from her as they returned to the house while he telephoned the garage. 'They'll collect it later today and return it tomorrow,' he told her. 'Shall we go?'

Such prompt service, thought Kristie, wasn't what she usually got. She always had to wait several days when she had any problems. But then, Radford was a man who got things done. One only had to look at him to see his overriding arrogance.

The kiss still loomed over them like a black cloud and as she sat silently beside him Kristie was conscious that their relationship had deteriorated. Not that there had been much of one in the beginning but it was even worse now.

And it was her fault. She shouldn't have called him a beast. Perhaps she ought to apologise? But by the time she had made the decision they were home and the moment was lost.

Chloe and Jake returned at the same time and Jake ran excitedly towards her. 'I didn't know it was you in that car,' he said. 'Whose is it?' His blue eyes widened with wonder at the big black limousine.

'It belongs to Mr Smythe. I work in his mother's house now.'

Radford got out of the car and smiled at Jake, going down on his haunches in front of him. 'Do you like it? Would you like a ride in it?'

'Oh, yes, please,' exclaimed Jake excitedly, forgetting his shyness when faced with this beautiful big car.

'You'll have to ask your mummy first.'

'Mummy, Mummy, can I?' he asked, hopping from one foot to the other, his eyes bright with excitement.

How could she say no in view of such enthusiasm? But, as she glanced from one face to the other, Kristie wasn't really thinking about her answer—she was looking for any signs of resemblance. And she couldn't think how she hadn't noticed before that their eyes, although one pair was blue and the other grey, were the same shape, even their eyebrows were the same. Not that Radford would notice, of course. He hadn't a clue that this was his son. She smiled grimly. Revenge was sweet.

'Can I, Mummy? Please say yes.'

'You can come with us,' said Radford, seeing her hesitation, guessing she was nervous about letting him out of her sight. 'Chloe too, if you like. But this young man—' he ruffled Jake's hair as he spoke '—is going to sit in the front and watch the controls for me. Isn't that right, son?'

Kristie knew it was a figure of speech, but hearing him

say 'son' sent a cold shiver down her spine. Already, though, she could see Jake's lip beginning to drop and knew she couldn't disappoint him. She raked up a huge smile. 'Of course.'

Radford grinned conspiratorially at Jake, as much as to say that he had known they would win. Effortlessly, he lifted the boy into the passenger seat, not leaving him until he had patiently fastened his seat-belt.

Kristie was stunned. These weren't the actions of a man who disliked children. But she had no time to dwell on it because Chloe was nudging her and whispering, 'What's going on with you and Mr Hunk?'

'Nothing,' hissed Kristie. 'Shut up. He'll hear you.'

'Tell me about it later.'

'There's nothing to tell,' insisted Kristie.

'Come on, you two,' Radford called out. 'This little boy is impatient to be off.'

They quickly slid into the back set, Chloe behind Jake and Kristie behind Radford, and the first thing she encountered were his eyes through the rear view mirror. She looked away but not before she had felt their full impact. She might have been mistaken but there seemed to be a challenge in those grey eyes and it made her faintly uneasy. Was he trying to tell her something, trying to prove that he did like children, perhaps? Or maybe he had put the act on for her benefit. Kristie didn't know what to think. All she knew was that she wanted to be out of this car as soon as possible.

Jake, on the other hand, couldn't sit still and his eyes were everywhere. 'What's this for? What's that? How does this work?' The questions came thick and fast and Radford patiently answered every one. But when Radford suggested they stop at McDonald's Kristie put her foot down.

'I don't encourage Jake to eat junk food,' she said

tightly. In fact, she was amazed that Radford would want to set foot in one of those places. High class restaurants were more his style.

'Now and then won't hurt him.'

'Maybe not, but the answer's still no.' She was glad when they returned home and relieved when Radford didn't get out of the car. She'd had the horrible feeling that he might invite himself into her house. 'What time shall I pick you up in the morning?' he asked.

'You don't have to do that,' she returned tightly. 'I'll get a lift off Chloe.'

'What's happened to your car?' asked the other girl as Kristie looked at her in anticipation.

Kristie grimaced. 'The starter motor's gone. Mr Smythe's getting it fixed for me.'

'Not something else!' exclaimed Chloe. 'You really ought to get yourself another one.'

It wasn't high on her list of priorities at the moment, although admittedly she had been thinking of it. But so long as her old Ford ran she didn't feel justified in spending money on another.

'And I can't give you a lift tomorrow because I have a dentist appointment.'

'Of course,' said Kristie. 'I'd forgotten.'

'So,' said Radford with a satisfied quirk to his lips, 'it looks as though my services will be needed after all. Shall we say eight forty-five?'

Kristie nodded silently and unhappily. She was spending far more time with this man than was good for her soul. There was a definite spark between them and if she wasn't careful it would ignite. But she must never forget what had happened to her sister. He didn't want a serious relationship with anyone or he would have been married long before now. He simply enjoyed playing the field. And she was his next target.

As soon as they were in the house Chloe slid her a meaningful glance. 'So what's going on between you two?'

'Who? Me and Mr Smythe? Absolutely nothing.'

'It's not what it looks like from my side of the fence.'

'You're imagining things, Chloe,' she declared shortly. 'He's not my type.'

'But he fancies you. I can tell from the way he looks at you.'

Kristie snorted indelicately. 'Radford knows how I feel about him.'

'So you have talked about feelings?' asked the other girl with a delighted smile. 'Or perhaps you've even—indulged?' she added with a wicked glint in her eyes.

Kristie couldn't stop the warmth that flooded her cheeks.

'So I'm right, he *has* kissed you. Tell me about it. What was it like? I bet he's the world's best kisser. He looks—'

'Shut up, Chloe!' cried Kristie. 'Go and get Jake his tea. I'm going to take a shower.'

Chloe waltzed into the kitchen singing about washing a man out of her hair and Kristie ran upstairs and slammed her bedroom door. The annoying thing was that Chloe was right.

After she'd showered and changed into a cool cotton pantsuit Kristie sat down with Jake while he had his tea. But even here the topic didn't change. All Jake could talk about was Mr Smythe and his car and when was he going to see him again? It was not until her son was in bed and fast asleep that Kristie began to relax.

The worst part was there would be more of the same tomorrow. It truly had been a fatal mistake moving her office.

When Paul phoned later he was the very antidote she

needed. There were no complications in their relationship and when he asked her to go out with him the following evening she willingly agreed. And the best thing was that if Radford tried to coerce her into dating him then she would have the perfect excuse.

It annoyed her that thoughts of Radford kept coming into her mind when she was doing her hardest to forget him. She flicked through the TV channels until she found a film that looked promising, but even then one of the characters looked faintly like Radford and she switched it off in disgust and went to bed.

Amazingly, she dropped straight off and slept dreamlessly, not waking until Jake jumped on her at seven-thirty the next morning. The three of them usually ate breakfast in the kitchen and today was no different. She totally ignored the few odd comments Chloe threw in about Radford, and when her son asked when he was going to see him again she shut him up as well.

'Mr Smythe's a very busy man, Jake. He only brought me home because my car wouldn't start.'

'But I like him. He said he'd take me out in his car again.'

Kristie frowned. She hadn't heard Radford say that. 'We'll have to see, won't we,' she said, silently vowing that it wouldn't happen if she had anything to do with it. She didn't want Radford anywhere near Jake.

Thankfully, when Radford came to pick her up Chloe and Jake had already left. Kristie was waiting and when she saw his car she hurried out of the house.

The very sight of Kristie walking towards him sent Radford's blood racing. Ever since yesterday, ever since he'd kissed her, he had been unable to get her out of his mind. She was beginning to grow on him far more than he had ever anticipated, despite the fact that she had accused him of mauling her. He'd been annoyed at the time but he knew that it had been a knee-jerk reaction. She was more angry with herself for allowing the kiss than with him for instigating it.

'Amazing, a woman who's ready on time,' he quipped, her beauty exciting him beyond measure. 'Good morning, Kristie. And it is a good morning, isn't it? The sun's shining, the birds are singing, and I have you in the car beside me. What more could a man ask for?'

Kristie totally ignored his comments, merely returning his greeting without any warmth.

Ouch, he thought. The kiss obviously still rankled. But he refused to be subdued. 'And how's the little man today?'

'Jake's fine,' she murmured.

'And yourself?'

'I'm all right too.'

'He enjoyed the ride. We'll have to do it again. Maybe we could take him to the seaside some time? I'm sure he'd enjoy that.'

If the flash of fire from Kristie's eyes had been real he'd have gone up in flames. This woman was full of fury, without a doubt. But he didn't see why it should be constantly projected at him. What had he done, for pity's sake? Maybe he resembled the guy who had hurt her. If that were so it could account for the way she'd reacted when they first met. But goodness, did she need to carry it on? He would never harm her the way this man had. Surely she could see that?

'I don't think that's a very good idea, Mr Smythe,' she told him icily.

He lifted his shoulders in what he hoped was an insouciant shrug, though in point of fact he was hurt by her rejection. 'It was just an idea. You needn't get on your high horse.'

Her stunning green eyes flashed again. 'I don't plan to have any kind of relationship with you.'

'And taking your son to the seaside constitutes a relationship, is that what you're saying?' His temper too began to rise.

'If I want Jake to see the sea then I'll take him myself.'

He gripped the wheel and willed himself not to say anything he would later regret. 'You're cutting off your nose to spite your face, you do know that? Why should your son miss out simply because of some misguided grudge you have against me?'

Kristie closed her eyes and he knew she was biting back a harsh response.

'But you needn't worry any further,' he went on. 'I'll consider the matter closed. I had a phone call from the garage. They're having trouble locating the spare for your car. It might be tomorrow before it's ready.'

He sensed her disappointment, guessed that half of it was directed at him. She didn't want to subject herself to any more lifts, she didn't want to sit in his car with him. Lord, it was painful having her think like this, and it made him all the more determined to prove that he was nothing like this man who had hurt her so much.

He very much needed a gently gently approach and he wasn't sure that he was up to it.

'We have a spare car languishing in one of the garages,' he told her now. 'You may use it if you like.' It would mean he wouldn't get to chauffeur her around but it wasn't doing him any good anyway, and she would probably think more of him for the offer.

'Whose is it?' she asked with a faint frown.

She was wearing a different perfume this morning, a little

more exotic than her usual one, more sophisticated. He wondered if subconsciously she was trying to tell him something. Perhaps that she was not a lady to be messed with? Whatever, he liked it and he found himself breathing more deeply so that he could imprint it in his memory.

'The car belongs to my mother. She bought a new one and kept that one for emergencies. I think I'd call this an emergency, wouldn't you? It's taxed and insured and thoroughly roadworthy. I'll sort the keys out and make sure it's ready for you.'

'I seem to be causing your family a lot of trouble,' she retorted. 'I should never have taken up your mother's offer in the first place.'

'But it's not my mother, is it? It's me. I remind you of Jake's father and you're determined to punish me for it. Isn't that so?' He glanced across at her and saw the look of guilt before she managed to hide it.

'If you know that why do you insist on making a nuisance of yourself?' she demanded heatedly.

'Because I am not Jake's father.' Heavens she was making this difficult. 'I am an entirely different man, and I take offence at being categorised.'

Kristie's eyes were pure ice as she looked at him. 'I have no wish to pursue this conversation.'

'Because you're losing, is that it?' They arrived at the gates to his family home and he turned towards her as he waited for them to open. 'You're doing yourself no favours, Kristie. Why don't you let yourself get to know me? You'll soon see that I'm nothing like—'

'You are *exactly* like him,' she retorted furiously. 'I'm going to tell your mother that having an office here is not working out.'

'And what reason will you give her?' he asked, his own

voice icily cold now. She was blowing this thing up out of all proportion.

Kristie gave a slow shrug. 'I'm not sure yet.'

'But not that it's because I remind you of someone you don't like? You know what she'd do if you said that, don't you? She'd tell me to go back to London. But I wouldn't. I'm determined to make you like me. One way or another, Kristie, you and I are going to become lovers.'

CHAPTER NINE

RADFORD'S threat made every one of Kristie's muscles bunch in protest. The thought of them becoming lovers both horrified and excited her at the same time. If she hadn't let him kiss her she would never have felt like this. She would have been totally sickened by the thought of him touching and kissing her. But that brief coming together of their lips had somehow whetted her appetite. It was a dreadful feeling and one that she knew she needed to banish to the deepest recesses of her mind.

But how? If he disappeared, if he returned to London and did the job he was supposed to be doing, then all would be well. He wasn't going to do that, though. He was going to stay here and torment her.

'You've gone very still,' he said to her now. 'The idea doesn't appeal, I take it?'

'Of course it doesn't appeal,' she riposted. 'And you know it. So why force yourself on me?'

'Oh, I won't force myself,' he said with the wickedest of smiles. 'I'll make very sure that you're ready for me.' The gates to his family home opened and he drove the car slowly through. 'In fact, I think part of the pleasure will be in persuading you that I'm not at all like your arch enemy.'

He was like a wolf ready for the kill with his lips bared back against his teeth and Kristie felt like spitting out the truth there and then, but there would be no joy in doing so. It would put an end to her plot and he would stake a claim in Jake, which was the last thing she wanted. So she returned his smile, even though it was lifeless and held no meaning.

'Very funny. It will take you a lifetime to do that, and I'm sure you wouldn't want to waste your energy on something so futile.'

'I don't happen to think it's futile. I happen to think that it would be relatively easy to get you to change your mind.'

Kristie sniffed and straightened her spine. 'Then you don't know the first thing about me.' As he slowed the car in front of her office she opened the door and jumped out. Without waiting to hear what his response would be, she took a short cut across the lawn—and almost pitched on her nose when her high heel sank into the grass.

She hissed out an expletive and tugged herself free, but not before she heard Radford's chuckle. And when she glanced back over her shoulder he was following her. 'What are you doing?' she rasped.

'I thought I'd enter the house this way.'

'Oh, no, you don't. This office is out of bounds. It's mine for as long as I work here.'

'I thought you were going to tell my mother you didn't want it any more?'

Kristie clenched her fists and didn't know what stopped her raining them against his chest. 'Maybe I will do just that. I've had enough of you.'

At that moment Felicity's wheelchair came trundling round the corner. 'Is this a stand-up fight? Can anyone watch?' She was grinning from ear to ear and appeared to be hugely enjoying herself. 'It looks like you've met your match, darling brother of mine.'

Kristie hid her embarrassment. 'I'd be obliged if you'd tell him to keep away from me,' she snapped.

'I don't think it will do any good.' His sister laughed.

'When Radford makes up his mind about something nothing stops him. He's finding you a challenge, Kristie.'

Kristie shook her head and turned her back on the two of them, opening the door with a shaking hand and making her way inside.

'I wanted to speak with you,' called out Felicity.

As there was no wheelchair access through this particular French window, Kristie was forced to come outside again. 'I'm sorry. I didn't realise.'

'I'll go and see how Mother is,' said Radford. 'She felt a migraine coming on. I'll see you later, Kristie. Hopefully we can do lunch again. Perhaps even a swim beforehand.'

It wasn't until he was out of sight that Kristie managed to relax enough to smile naturally at his sister.

'He can be very trying,' suggested Felicity.

Kristie didn't want to say too much because he was her beloved brother after all. 'I'm not sure that—'

'He wants a relationship and you don't. That's it, isn't it?' Felicity's lovely grey eyes looked directly at Kristie. 'And he's being his usual bullying self. I guessed you were the reason he didn't go back to London straight away. He homed in on you the moment he saw you. Which is unusual for him. He usually takes his time. He likes to get to know a girl from a distance before he makes his move.'

Kristie didn't believe that. Tarah had given her the impression that it had been love at first sight when the two of them had met. He hadn't watched her from a distance, that was for sure.

'You obviously have something the other girls haven't had.'

'So how many have there been?' Kristie said with a frown.

Felicity's fine brows lifted. 'Who knows what he gets up to in London?'

'Has he brought any of them here?'

'To meet my mother?' Felicity laughed. 'Not likely, though they do phone him. But his type is not my mother's type—except for you, of course,' she added with a sly grin.

'What do you mean?' Kristie said jerkily. Surely they hadn't been discussing her as potential wife material? How humiliating. Everything was getting worse.

'Don't worry. My mother hasn't said a thing. It's simply that I know her, and I've seen the way she looks at you and Radford when you're together. I wouldn't be surprised if it wasn't why she offered you an office here.'

Kristie's heart began to beat uncomfortably fast. It looked as though she really had walked into this one. And there was no way out without upsetting Peggy, which she didn't want to do, not at this stage anyway.

'I don't want anything to do with your brother,' she said quietly now, 'and I don't want to talk about him any more.'

'That's a pity. I'd like you as my sister-in-law. It's all right,' she added quickly, seeing Kristie's shocked face. 'I'm on your side. I could put a word in for you if you like. He shouldn't make a nuisance of himself if you don't—'

'I can manage my own affairs,' said Kristie quickly. 'What was it you wanted to see me about?'

Felicity grimaced. 'I've changed my mind about the design of the earrings for the bridesmaids. You haven't commissioned them yet?'

And so the subject of Radford was safely pushed to one side and Kristie spent her morning quietly without any further interruptions. Except in her mind, of course. How could she work here and not have him pop into her thoughts at all too frequent intervals? Even thinking about him sent her hormone levels rising. Thank goodness she was seeing Paul tonight, everything would be normal again. She could completely forget Radford and concentrate on this man who had been a major part of her life for the last twelve months.

There were no ups and downs with Paul; he was a solid, calming influence. Even if she had business worries he made her see that there was a way out. Nothing was ever as bad as she imagined when Paul was around. She was looking forward to their dinner date very much.

A phone call took her away before lunch, much to her relief. Peggy's car had been got ready and the keys brought to her. It was bigger and newer than her own car but very easy to drive and she spent the afternoon discussing details for another glitzy wedding. She was going to have her work cut out these coming months and would need every little bit of help Chloe could give her.

She had already thought about networking her two computers so that she could work in either place, and she felt that this was now becoming a necessity. In fact it might be better to move back so that Chloe could work with her when Jake was at school. On the other hand, she wouldn't have all her lovely new equipment which really was a boon.

She was home before Jake finished school and she took the opportunity to have a long soak in a fragrant bath. It was heaven. And before Paul came to pick her up she was able to spend a couple of precious hours with her darling son.

'What have you been doing at school today, darling?' she asked as she cuddled him after his bath. He felt soft and sweet and warm and she loved him so very much.

To her amazement tears came to his eyes. 'My friends made Father's Day cards. I couldn't because I don't have a daddy. Joshua said I must have one because everyone has a daddy. So who is mine? Is it Paul?'

Kristie's throat closed and her eyes grew moist too. 'No, darling, it isn't Paul.' It looked as though the time was fast

approaching when she would need to tell him the truth
about his birthright. She had always thought he would be
much older before he began asking questions, more able to
understand. And she hadn't really prepared herself.

'But I want a daddy.'

'I know you do, sweetheart.' Kristie held him even
tighter. 'We'll have to see what we can do about it, won't
we?'

And for the moment that seemed to appease him.

He was in bed before Paul arrived, giving Kristie the
time she needed to compose herself. It had upset her, hearing Jake ask about his daddy.

'I adore you in that colour,' said Paul, looking admir-
ingly at her lilac dress and jacket. 'I'm looking forward to
tonight. I've booked us a table at The Manor. Is that all
right?'

'Perfect.' He was always solicitous of her needs, often
consulting her before he made a choice. Unlike Radford,
who took complete control and expected everyone else to
fall in with his plans. And why had he sprung into mind?
This was supposed to be a Radford-free evening. She
wanted to enjoy herself; she wanted to relax and have fun.

The Manor was a place they'd used many times before.
As the name suggested, it was an old manor house, once
in a state of decay but now restored to its former splendour.
It was on the outskirts of Stratford-upon-Avon, with its
lawns running down to the banks of the river.

Even though it was mid-summer it wasn't warm enough
to sit outside but they had a window seat with splendid
views of the water and the swans. 'I've been looking forward to this,' said Kristie once they were settled at their
table.

'Me too,' he agreed. 'How long's it been since we last
had dinner out?'

Kristie couldn't remember. 'Time flies. And I've picked up another client today. I'm going to be so busy it's unbelievable.'

'Is it working out, this new office lark?'

'It's good,' Kristie assured him.

'It seems a bit stupid to me, all this to-ing and fro-ing when you were quite comfortable at home.'

'Not at all. There's such a lot of useful equipment.' She didn't tell him that it had been bought especially for her. 'It makes life a lot easier. How about your work? Are you still as busy as ever?' She felt sure that his next question would be about Radford and she wanted to forestall him.

Paul talked right through their first course. 'People constantly amaze me,' he said. 'Some of them are oblivious that their lives are in danger. Faulty wiring is one of the culprits. But enough about me. Tell me about this new job you've picked up.'

They chatted animatedly right through the meal. It was like old times before Radford came on the scene, thought Kristie. She felt comfortable with Paul. Nothing ever disturbed her when they were together. It was an easy, uncomplicated relationship.

'Do you see much of Radford?' he asked casually as they waited for their coffee.

'He pops home occasionally,' she admitted. 'But he's mostly in London.' She prayed forgiveness for the little white lie, and she wished with all her heart that Paul hadn't brought his name into the conversation. She hadn't felt this relaxed in a long time.

'And when he's home does he offer to take you out?'

'Paul,' she pleaded, 'let's not discuss Radford tonight. I'm really enjoying myself. I don't want anything to spoil it.'

'And Radford would spoil it?'

'Yes,' she declared emphatically.

'There's nothing going on between you?'

'Most definitely not.'

He smiled then. 'I'm glad because—well, because I—' All of a sudden he seemed unsure of himself. And then he fished a small leather box out of his pocket and, opening it he took out a diamond ring. 'Because, Kristie—will you marry me?'

CHAPTER TEN

RADFORD had been looking forward to a swim with Kristie and was bitterly disappointed when he discovered that she'd disappeared without telling him. He'd eaten a very lonely lunch because his mother and Felicity had gone out, and then spent all afternoon waiting for Kristie to return.

When she didn't he began to wonder whether she was staying away because of him. Was he wasting his time? Ought he to go back to London and forget her? But how could he banish her from his thoughts when she filled them every waking hour? She was the most intriguing woman he'd ever met—so much so that he lay awake at night imagining her in bed beside him.

He even dreamt about her—the most fantastic dreams where their lovemaking transported him to the edge and beyond. He always awoke feeling blissfully happy, only to sink into depression when he realised that it had all been a dream and was unlikely to ever come true.

Not that he was going to give up trying, but his hopes weren't high. Kristie Swift was an aggressively determined woman who, once her mind was made up, didn't change it. And she had certainly made up her mind about him. Right from the word go. He would never forget the look she had given him when they had first met. Shock, horror, distaste. And for what reason? Because he looked like another man. What did he have to do to convince her that he was nothing like that person? Why wouldn't she give him a chance to prove it?

He waited until he guessed she had put Jake to bed and

then he rang her, but it was Chloe who answered and disappointment welled. He had looked forward to hearing Kristie's lovely melodious voice, had even felt a stirring of his hormones as he dialled the number. 'It's Radford.'

'Hello.' Her voice was slightly breathless and he smiled to himself. He hadn't failed to notice that she seemed smitten by him.

'How are you?' he asked.

'I'm—fine.' She clearly hadn't expected that question.

'And how's Jake?'

'He's fast asleep.'

'In that case, do you think I could have a word with his mother, please?'

'I'm sorry,' Chloe said huskily. 'She's not here.'

He frowned. 'She's not still working, surely?'

There was a slight hesitation, then, 'She's gone out to dinner with Paul.'

Damn! The very thought of her spending time with the other man sent streaks of jealousy through his brain. 'I see. Thank you. Tell her I've called, will you?' He didn't realise how clipped his tones were.

'Is there a message?' asked Chloe.

'No, nothing. I'll see her tomorrow.' And he slammed down the phone. He shouldn't have left it so late in the day. He recalled the way she'd kissed Paul, a full on kiss with her body pressed close to his. And now she'd gone out with him for some intimate dinner for two. How often did this happen? Was he being a fool?

There had definitely been a faint response that time he had kissed her—and if she loved Paul there wouldn't have been, would there? He asked himself the question but wasn't sure of the answer.

In his mind's eye he saw the two of them enjoying a candlelit dinner in some secluded place. He saw her responding to Paul. He saw her touching his hand, stroking, caressing. He saw them lean towards each other and kiss. He saw the love in her eyes.

And he felt bitterness rise in his throat. Tomorrow, he determined, he would begin an all out attack. He couldn't risk losing her.

As soon as he saw her arrive for work the following morning he went along to her office and knocked on the door. He didn't even attempt to open it because he knew he would find it locked. It always was.

When she let him in he found himself studying her face intently to see whether she'd spent a night of passion.

'Is something wrong?' she asked sharply. 'Is my mascara smudged?'

'Not at all.' She certainly didn't look like a woman who'd been well and truly made love to, so perhaps there was hope after all. If she was his woman she'd go around with a smile on her face all the time; he'd make sure of that. There wouldn't be a moment when she wasn't thinking about him and the excitement of their lovemaking.

'Chloe told me you phoned last night,' she said irritably. 'Why?'

'I wanted to take you out.'

A delicate eyebrow lifted and she shook her head and laughed, a light trickle of sound that feathered along his nerves. 'You don't give up, I'll hand you that, but you don't really think I'd have agreed?'

He knew deep in his heart that she wouldn't, but he wasn't going to admit it. Never before had he wanted a woman as desperately as he did Kristie now. Simply standing here looking at her made his heart rain hammer blows within his chest, and every male hormone he possessed ran rampant through his body.

'How are we ever going to resolve our differences if you won't spend time with me?' he asked.

Her eyes flashed scathingly. 'Hasn't it occurred to you that I don't want to be friends? That I don't want to sort things out?'

'Hmph!' he snorted. 'You're sticking your head in the sand instead of facing your problems head on. I won't go along with it. I want to prove to you that I'm not out to cause harm. Why don't you tell me what your bad experience was?'

Alarm filled her eyes and she looked at him in horror and he almost wished he hadn't said anything.

'I was wrong to ask. You don't have to tell me,' he said quickly. 'It clearly still hurts very much; but put yourself in my shoes. How do you think I feel when I see fear and hatred in your eyes every time you look at me?'

Kristie shrugged. 'You know the answer to that, don't you? Go back to London. I don't know why you're hanging around anyway.'

She really knew how to turn the knife. Why the hell was he bothering? Why didn't he do as she said?

Because he loved her!

The thought hit him like a punch in the stomach. How had that happened? How could he love such a woman? The answer was clear. Love happened whether you wanted it to or not. It took nothing into account. And he had fallen hook, line and sinker for Kristie Swift. The only female he had ever met who hated his guts from the word go. Challenge wasn't the word for it. It went deeper than that. He was desperate to change her mind. And nothing or no one was going to stop him.

'I shall stay for as long as I like,' he told her, his eyes firm and steady on hers. 'Faint heart never won fair lady, isn't that what they say?'

'Maybe, but faint or strong it makes no difference. You'll be wasting your time. Paul's asked me to marry him.'

Another body blow! And this one was entirely unexpected. He took a deep breath and fought the anger that came over him. She couldn't marry this man—he wouldn't let her. He would fight every inch of the way, dirty if he had to.

His eyes blazed with a passion she had not yet seen, but one that would be very much to the fore in the future. 'Until I see his wedding ring on your finger I shall see you as fair game.'

'You can't do that,' she retorted with very real fury in her eyes.

'Can't I? Believe me, I can and I will.' His nostrils flared as he fought for control. Getting angry with her wasn't the answer. It was no way to win her over. He had thought he would do it gradually, but that wasn't going to work now. It had to be action all the way.

It had been an error of judgement, letting Radford think she was going to marry Paul. She had thought it would get him off her back; instead she had made the situation worse. In truth, she hadn't yet given Paul his answer. It was one great big dilemma. Jake needed a father and he loved Paul. But she didn't love Paul. Would marrying him be the biggest mistake of her life?

The most disturbing thought of all was that if Radford hadn't come on the scene then she might have said yes. She might have married him for Jake's sake, and that wouldn't have been fair on Paul.

Radford was the last man in the whole country she wanted anything to do with and yet that one brief kiss had shown her how easy it would be to fall for his undisputed charm. Even now, standing here glaring at him, she couldn't fail to be aware of the strong electrical impulses that were shooting between them.

It was as though he had knocked a switch and turned the booster on. And when he took a meaningful step towards her she lost all power in her arms and legs. Even her throat locked tight and she was unable to speak. Her eyes were the only thing that moved. She stared at him in increasing fear because she knew that he was about to kiss her and she would be unable to stop him.

His smile was slow and sexy and his eyes as dark as a midnight sky. She castigated herself because she was doing nothing. Her heart became a thumping mass when he got so close that she could smell the intoxicating maleness of him and feel the heat of a body that was aching for love.

Kristie closed her eyes because she didn't want to see any more; she didn't want to feel any more. This was a nightmare happening while she was awake; something over which she had no control. His lips, when they touched hers, were warm and firm and light. She could have broken free any second she wanted, but she didn't. When his arms came around her they too were gentle. The bonds were of her own making.

As he urged her against his body she could feel an echoing rapid thud in his chest; it was almost as though their two hearts were drumming as one. His gentle persuasion soon had her melting in his arms and when he deepened the kiss, when he gained access to her mouth with his tongue, she could no more have rejected him than she could have dived to the bottom of the deepest ocean.

Paul, and her promise to give him his answer soon, was the last thing on her mind. As Radford's kisses became more urgent and demanding Kristie found herself kissing him back. She couldn't stop herself. Something incredibly powerful was happening inside her. So powerful that it took precedence over everything else. Sensations such as she had never experienced before tore through her body like an express train, sending a red-hot fever through her limbs and an urgent moistness between her legs.

Alarmingly, Radford seemed to know exactly how she felt. He began murmuring words of encouragement as knowing fingers touched first one and then the other tightly peaked breast, the silky top she wore and the gossamer bra providing little resistance. And when she didn't stop him, when she groaned her approval, wriggling her hips ecstatically against his, he lowered his head and sucked her nipples through the fine material.

The sensations he aroused were incredible; she was fast reaching fever pitch—and every one of them zoned in to one area of her body. Never in a million years would Paul have managed to stir her to this extent. If she married him she would be stuck in an unexciting union. Life would follow a mundane pattern. They would perhaps make love once a week, but other than that they would simply be friends. If Radford was doing nothing else, he was opening her eyes in this direction.

When Kristie reached out and touched Radford's manhood—was it need that drove her or curiosity?—she realised that she was in danger of spinning out of control. It had happened almost without her being aware of it. Radford had the power to make her do things that she didn't want to do. She could see why Tarah had enthused over him.

As she thought of her sister Kristie suddenly realised that she was letting The Enemy make love to her and she froze. Before she knew it she would be letting him have his evil way. She could even get pregnant. Another bastard child to bring into the world. Because she knew without a shadow of doubt that Radford would hot-tail it back to London if ever that happened. Not that she would want him to marry her. No, thank you. Not on those terms. Not ever.

With a brilliant flash of her green eyes she worked her hands up between them and pushed hard on his chest. 'What the hell are you doing? Get away from me. I don't want this. Don't touch me again, ever.'

To give him his due, he stepped back but he frowned in confusion. 'Kristie, I wasn't—'

'Wasn't what?' she snapped. 'Trying to take advantage? Of course you were. It's what you've been after ever since we met. And don't try to deny it.' Lord, she felt awful, she'd been in danger of spinning out of control. This man who thought he was God's gift had almost got her eating out of his hand. How he'd managed it she wasn't sure. But somehow she had taken leave of her senses. She'd actually touched him! The very thought made a fresh rage of heat tear through her body.

She shook her head wildly, red hair flying, green eyes sparking. 'Get out of here.'

'You don't mean that.' In contrast, he was calm and controlled, leaning back on the edge of her desk as though they were having a perfectly normal conversation. His very calmness served to enrage her further.

'Don't I?' she spat. 'The truth is I never want to see you again.'

'You're angry because you let your heart rule your head for once. It's something you've schooled yourself against for so long that now it's happening it's scaring you. Tell me I'm wrong.'

'You're wrong.' But she was lying, and he knew it. She was scared by the depth of emotions he had managed to arouse. She was attracted to him far more than was good for her. It was this she was fighting now, and she was so scared that she wanted to run away. She really had pinned herself into a corner here in this beautiful house. Nothing was going according to plan.

'I'll go,' he growled softly. 'But don't think you've seen the last of me.' His eyes never left hers as he moved towards the door, stirring her senses still further but increasing her anger at the same time. And then he smiled, a wicked, primeval smile. 'This is only the beginning, lover.'

Lover? What an exciting thought. How she would love to share her bed with him. But it was impossible. Whatever was happening to her body and mind she had to put his treatment of Tarah first. She needed to make very sure that nothing like that happened to her. In fact, she wouldn't let him into her office. If she rejected him often enough he would get the message and go back to London. Or was that wishful thinking? She hadn't failed to discover that Radford Smythe was one very determined man, and unfortunately he had his sights set on her.

Why she remained in her office for the rest of the day Kristie didn't know. It was impossible to concentrate on work, even though she did her very best. Images of Radford kept forming in her mind's eye.

Radford the hated enemy!

Radford the perfect lover!

The heat rushed to her skin every time she thought along these lines, but she couldn't stop herself.

Paul had kissed her last night. A long, lingering kiss which she'd found very pleasant. Not exciting, not exhilarating, just pleasant. Nevertheless, she had almost convinced herself that she was in love with him and that marrying him would be the answer to everything.

It had troubled her, Jake asking about his daddy. Marrying Paul would put an end to such fears. Even the fact that Jake had asked her if Paul was his daddy should have told her something. Paul was the only male in his life and they got on well—like father and son, in fact. Why not cement the relationship?

But then Radford's kiss would rise like a phoenix from the ashes. It would fly in her face, tormenting her, telling her that she would never be happy with Paul, that he would never make her feel truly woman, senseless with desire, hungry for everything that he had to offer.

No, that couldn't be true. Radford was her enemy—he was the man who had caused Tarah's death. She hated him from the bottom of her heart. She did. *She did!* But it was getting harder to convince herself of the fact.

From the corner of her eye she saw Radford strolling across the lawn towards the swimming pool. She moved closer to the window. All he wore was a pair of brief black swimming trunks with a towel flung over one shoulder. And what a gorgeous body he had. She couldn't take her eyes off him.

His legs were long and muscular, his back broad and well muscled, his waist and hips narrow, skin firm and tanned. Just watching him sent a flurry of sensation to the very heart of her. He walked with the lithe grace of a feral animal, and all of a sudden he turned his head and gave a brief wave. Surely he hadn't seen her watching him?

But clearly he had. He must have sensed it, and Kristie drew back with a jerk, the blood rushing to her cheeks. There was no way on this earth that she wanted Radford to think that she was interested in him. Because she wasn't. Not in the slightest.

Or so she tried to convince herself. In truth, he had insinuated himself not only into her mind but her heart as well and he was there to stay for all eternity. It was frightening. Because of what had happened to her sister she ought to have more sense, and yet still she couldn't help herself.

It was time to make a dash for it. To pack up and leave while he was in the pool and could do nothing about it. Or was that the coward's way out? She decided it was, and so for the next hour she forced herself to get on with her work and not think about him. To a certain degree she was successful.

When she finally ventured out to her borrowed car Radford was nowhere in sight, and as she drove round the house she saw that his car was not on the drive at the front either. It was as though a weight had lifted from her shoulders and she sang to herself on the journey home.

Her good mood didn't last long. When she arrived, the first thing she saw was Radford's sleek black car parked outside her house. Everything inside her burst into angry life and she banged the door open and marched inside.

There was no one about. Then she heard the sound of Jake's laughter coming from the garden. A glance through the kitchen window revealed a breathless Jake chasing after a football which Radford dribbled around the lawn. Jake was pulling and tugging at Jake's legs and Chloe was watching and clapping her hands.

Kristie stormed outside. 'What's going on?' she demanded, arms akimbo, eyes flashing furiously at Radford.

'We're having a game of football.'

'I can see that, but what are you doing here?'

'Waiting for you.'

'Why?' She couldn't say too much in front of Jake, but she sure as hell would have a lot to say to him when they were alone. Meanwhile, Jake came running towards her, laughing as she gathered him in her arms.

'Come and play with us,' he begged. 'We're having lots of fun.'

Kristie didn't want to play football with Radford; she didn't want him here, full stop. He was taking a liberty turning up like this in her absence—not that Jake or Chloe seemed to mind; they were having a ball.

Chloe couldn't take her eyes off Radford and now she looked from him to Kristie, giving a helpless shrug as Kristie glared.

'I don't want to play, darling,' she said to Jake. 'I've had a busy day and I'm going to take a shower.' As he ran off to get his ball she turned to Radford with a grim expression. 'I shall expect you to be gone when I come down.'

He spread his hands. 'Why? When the sole purpose of my visit was to see you.'

'Whatever you have to say can wait until tomorrow,' she told him coldly. 'In fact, I can't see why you couldn't have spoken to me earlier. There was no need for this.'

'It's not exactly words I'm after,' he growled in a voice too low for the others to hear.

Kristie felt as though an elastic band had been twanged inside her, reverberating through her veins at a tremendous rate, but, curse it, this wasn't what she wanted. She wanted to put a million miles between them—for ever! Either that or she wanted to hurt him as he had hurt her sister. Keeping from him the fact that Jake was his son didn't seem to be enough any more. What he didn't know didn't bother him. And she wanted him to feel pain.

'I can't believe you said that, right here in front of my son,' she hissed through closed teeth. 'What sort of a crazed maniac are you?'

A flash of anger narrowed his eyes. 'I'm neither crazy nor a maniac. I'm simply a man with very human desires.'

And at this moment he desired her! 'And you think that making advances to me in front of Jake is the right thing to do?' She kept her voice down but her whole face was a mask of displeasure and out of the corner of her eye she could see Chloe watching them. Once Radford had gone she would be subjected to the third degree and Chloe would never be able to understand why she was spurning Radford's advances.

It wasn't her intention, though, to tell Chloe the truth. What Radford had done to Tarah was far too close to her heart to share it with Jake's babysitter. Because that was really all she was. She wasn't her close friend and confidante; she was her paid employee. There were times when it didn't feel like that, times when they huddled together in girlie conversation and had a good laugh. But some things were private, and this was one of them.

'Advances?' he asked harshly. 'I wasn't aware that's what I'm doing.'

'Suggestions, then,' she grated. 'You had no right coming here and you know it.'

'Jake was pleased to see me.'

Kristie closed her eyes for a couple of seconds, praying that this was all a bad dream and when she opened them again he would be gone. But no such luck. He was there right in front of her, larger than life. A gorgeously handsome man with compelling dark eyes who, under other circumstances, she would have fallen instantly in love with. 'Jake is pleased to see anyone who'll play with him,' she retorted.

'Or who has a smart car that he'd love another ride in. In fact, I've promised him one. I said we'd all go to McDonald's for tea.'

'You've what?' Kristie's voice rose shrilly, causing both Jake and Chloe to look at her curiously. She lowered her voice again angrily. 'You had no right.' Lord, the man was taking over.

'Well, I'm sorry, but the deed's done. Promises can't be broken, especially to a child. Chloe said you had no plans for tonight.'

'Chloe doesn't know everything,' she retorted. 'Paul will probably call round.' Which was an outright lie because Paul was going to visit his parents in Cheltenham. He'd wanted her to go with him, perhaps hoping that she might give him her decision and they could tell his mother and father that they were engaged, but Kristie had declined to go. She wanted more time to think; she didn't want to be rushed into things.

'You're not wearing his ring yet,' Radford pointed out, looking deliberately at her bare finger. 'So in my eyes it makes you fair game.'

'You'd steal another man's girlfriend?'

'Only if I thought they weren't right together.'

Kristie threw him a scathing glance. 'And what sort of an excuse is that? A pretty poor one, if you ask me.'

'So you're going to let Jake down?'

This was emotional blackmail and Kristie's heart sank like a lead weight into the pit of her stomach. 'You know I wouldn't do that.'

His smile was triumphant. 'Run along and get your shower, then. I'll be waiting.' And his words held more than a hint of promise.

Radford had never been in a McDonald's before and didn't expect to like it very much. But needs must, he had thought. He wanted Jake on his side. With the boy's enthusiasm and the woman he loved sitting opposite him where he could watch every expression on her lovely face, every movement of those incredible green eyes, he enjoyed himself as much as if he'd been dining in a five-star hotel. Perhaps more, because Jake's enthusiasm was infectious and he was seeing things through a young person's eyes for the very first time.

He'd never bothered much with children, had never really wanted any of his own—probably because his cousin's two children were holy terrors. But if he had a son as well-behaved and as polite as Jake, then perhaps it wouldn't be so bad after all. He found himself watching Kristie's son even more intently.

He could see a faint resemblance, but only very faint; he obviously took after his father. Simply thinking about the man who had hurt Kristie so much tightened every muscle in his body. She didn't deserve that. He wanted to care for her; he wanted to reassure her that not all men were the same. It was an underhand trick, trying to do it through her son, but if it worked then it would be worth it.

Although Kristie laughed and appeared to be having a good time, he was aware that she resented every second of his presence. She tried not to talk to him if she could help it, but Jake drew them both into his conversation, as did Chloe. Chloe was a funny little thing but she had told him confidentially while they were waiting for Kristie to come home that she wished Kristie could find herself a good man. And he had read into it that she meant he could be the one. Not Paul. He wondered if she knew that Paul had proposed to Kristie?

Kristie hadn't actually told him whether she had said yes or no. She'd given the impression of agreeing, but he had a sneaky feeling it wasn't true. Otherwise she'd surely be wearing his ring?

When they got back to Kristie's house he didn't give her the chance to say thank you very much and goodbye. He hoisted Jake up on to his shoulders when they got out of the car and marched to the door.

'Can we play football again?' asked Jake, loving his lofty perch.

Kristie answered for him. 'I don't think so. It's time for bed.'

Jake pulled a face.

Radford said, 'Just five minutes, then you must do as Mummy says.'

Kristie glared. Even that was too much. But Radford smiled and proceeded into the house when she opened the door, stooping so as not to bang Jake's head, carrying him right through into the garden, where the boy raced around like a mad thing.

Five minutes passed in no time but it wasn't in Radford's mind to leave when Jake was called in. Oh, no, he intended to spend the evening with Kristie. He followed her into the house. The way she had reacted to him that morning had told him a great deal about this young lady's feelings.

He had been pleasantly surprised when she had responded. In fact, pleasant didn't begin to describe it. He'd been ebullient because it had proved she wasn't immune to him. She might verbally attack him but her body told another story; it had no way of keeping up her defences. And tonight he meant to press home his advantage. Chloe had already told him that it was her night off, so there would be no one to interrupt them. And he certainly hadn't believed Kristie when she had said that Paul might pop round; it had been an excuse for his benefit.

'I'll bath Jake while you talk to Radford,' Chloe said pleasantly, winking to Radford behind Kristie's back.

He waited for the expected refusal and was pleasantly surprised when none came, but he soon found that it didn't mean she was agreeable to him staying. She simply wanted Jake out of earshot.

'What do you mean, walking into my house like this?' she demanded as soon as they were alone.

'Aren't you pleased to see me?'

'No, I am not,' she countered furiously.

'Methinks the lady doth protest too much.'

'With just cause,' she snapped.

He lifted a sceptical brow. 'If you're not interested in me, tell me, why were you watching me through your office window this afternoon? Tell me you weren't excited seeing my naked body. I know I would have been if I'd seen yours. We really must take a swim together some time.'

'Over my dead body,' she riposted, as he had known she would. 'And I wasn't watching you—I happened to glance out of the window, that's all.'

'I see.'

'No, you don't. You don't see anything,' she flared, angry because he was smiling. And he had good cause to smile. The greater her denial, the more likely it was that he'd hit on the truth. Especially as her cheeks had gone a delicate shade of pink.

'I see more than you think,' he said. 'May I congratulate you on the way you've brought up your son. He does you credit.'

To his amazement, she flushed further. 'I do my best.'

'More than that, considering you run your own business as well.'

'It troubles me sometimes that I have to leave him,' she admitted.

'But you have a treasure in Chloe and, as far as I can see, Jake hasn't suffered by your absences.'

'Perhaps. But he didn't suffer at all when I worked from home,' she reproached him.

His eyes narrowed. 'Are you blaming me or my mother? You didn't have to accept her offer.'

'No, I didn't,' she answered sharply. 'And there are times when I wish I hadn't.'

'Yes, I know. But on the whole I imagine it's working out very well?'

'I love all the new equipment,' she admitted. 'It's a great help. I presume you had a hand in that?'

He inclined his head. 'I tried to think of everything, but if there's—'

She stopped him quickly. 'No! Your family's already been more than generous.'

'It's because my mother likes you. You'd really upset her if you left. You do know that?'

'Of course. But it wouldn't upset me if you left now. You're outstaying your welcome.'

'I'm sorry you feel like that.' It had taken her longer than he expected. He had thought he must be making progress. 'But the whole point of me coming was to spend time with you,' he argued. There was no way on this earth that he was going to leave.

'Why? In any case, as I've told you, Paul will be here later.'

'Then I'll stay till he comes,' he said, calling her bluff.

He watched the battle she had with herself, a battle she lost. A whole host of conflicting emotions crossed her face—everything from anger and resentment to final acceptance of the inevitable.

'You're wasting your time,' she said in a dull, flat voice.

'I don't think so, but if I am, then that's my worry, not yours. Ah, here's Jake all clean and ready for bed. Have you come for a goodnight kiss, young man?'

Jake grinned and ran across to him, clambering on to his lap as though he had always known him.

Radford hugged the boy and was surprised by the depth of feeling that welled up inside him. This was a totally new experience. 'You have a good night's sleep, Jake.'

'Will you come and read to me?'

He glanced across at Kristie and caught her appalled

look. 'Perhaps another time,' he said, letting the boy slide to the floor, watching him as he ran across to his mother.

'Will *you* read me a story, Mummy?'

'Of course, sweetheart.' She stood up and took his hand. 'Say ni-night to Mr Smythe.'

'Ni-night,' said Jake obediently, 'and thank you for taking me out.'

'You're welcome, son.'

The room was silent after they'd left. Chloe was still upstairs, probably getting herself ready to go out, and he was alone with his thoughts. If he ruined things tonight then he could kiss goodbye to any sort of a relationship with Kristie. It was, he felt, a make or break time.

CHAPTER ELEVEN

RADFORD could faintly hear Kristie as she read to her son. As always her voice made his skin prickle; it was truly beautiful. Without stopping to think what he was doing, he crept up the stairs following the musical sound. He paused in the doorway to Jake's room and held his breath at the vision of Kristie sitting on a chair at the side of the bed.

A sunbeam stole through a slit in the curtains and highlighted her hair. She looked Madonna-like in her beauty and the sight of Jake's rapt little face as he watched her, his eyes gradually closing, would remain with him for ever. It was the perfect mother and child picture. Full of love. His heart ached suddenly for a child of his own who would look at him like that.

With a lump in his throat he turned and padded softly back down the stairs, and when Kristie returned he was sitting in the same seat as before, his eyes closed. He opened them when she spoke his name.

'I thought you were asleep,' she said, still in that same lovely voice. He wanted her to read a story to him. It was silly, he knew, but he wanted her to sit beside him and recite something, anything, just so that he could listen to her. It wouldn't send him to sleep, though, like it did Jake. It would excite and arouse.

'Would you like a drink?' she asked. 'A coffee perhaps, or some beer?'

Beer! Paul's beer undoubtedly. 'No, thank you.' He wasn't a beer person; he preferred Scotch. But not when he was driving. 'I'd love a coffee. Shall I make it?' And, without waiting for her answer, he jumped to his feet. 'Come and show me where everything is.'

The white kitchen was sleek and uncluttered and he couldn't help but admire her very orderly life. Not that he could work in a mess himself; he couldn't, but he remembered how shocked he had been when he had first seen Kristie's minimalist living room. But, having sat there for the best part of half an hour, he was surprised how much it had begun to grow on him.

'I only have instant, I'm afraid,' she said.

'That's all right; I'm an instant fan. Living alone has taught me to do things the easy way. Now my mother; she wouldn't thank you for instant coffee. It has to be the very finest of beans, which she grinds herself. Or, to be correct, whoever's making the coffee grinds them. I've heard Cook complain more than once when she's been particularly busy and my mother's demanded coffee. It's the same with her tea. No tea bags for her, oh, no. Loose tea made the old-fashioned way. My mother has standards to keep, you know.'

Kristie laughed, as he had intended she should, and he filled the kettle while she reached out mugs and spoons and the coffee and sugar jars. It was a cosy, domesticated scene and he wondered if she felt the same, or whether she was still wishing he would do a disappearing act.

He turned to face her while waiting for the kettle to boil. 'Is it really so bad, having me in your house?' he asked, deliberately keeping his voice seductively low.

Kristie avoided looking at him. 'I suppose not,' she murmured, though not very convincingly.

'So long as I toe the line? Is that what you're thinking?' She nodded.

'I can't promise that, Kristie. You know how I feel about

you and, if you're honest, you're not entirely immune to me either.'

She closed her eyes and a shudder ran through her. 'That's the whole trouble,' she said, more to herself than to him.

He hid a smile. Her defences were cracking. 'And it wouldn't be playing the game if you were unfaithful to Paul? Or is it because you still class me the same as that monster who screwed you up and you're afraid that if you let yourself even so much as like me you'll get more of the same treatment?'

Dammit, he shouldn't have said that. He shouldn't have said anything that would spoil the harmony of the moment. He didn't want her thinking harsh thoughts, only good ones. But, as it happened, he had no idea what she was thinking because she didn't answer him. 'The kettle's boiling,' she said instead, and he gave her some breathing space while he filled the mugs.

When he turned around she had gone outside, so he took the coffee to her and they sat on a wooden bench. It had been a hot midsummer's day and was still pleasantly warm. Her garden was long and neatly lawned with a few shrubs around the edges. There was a swing and a slide for Jake, and the heavy fragrance of a honeysuckle growing against the house wall filled the air around them.

For a while they sat in silence, each busy with their own thoughts, but sitting so close without touching her was the hardest thing he had ever done. He was so conscious of her that it hurt and he drank his coffee scalding hot in an attempt to give himself something to do.

He desperately wanted to put his hand on her leg, or round her shoulders, and draw her close. Any sort of contact would be welcome. This was sheer purgatory. 'How long have you lived here?' he asked at last. God, what a stupid question. Did he really want to know? He should have said, I want to kiss you, I want to make love to you; I want you to love me too.

How would she have taken that? he wondered. With fright probably. She'd have got up and put as much space between them as possible.

'About five years,' she said quietly. 'I moved here after Jake was born. I lived in a flat before then. It was no place to bring up a child.'

This was the most she had ever disclosed about herself and he was surprised, but before he could say anything else Chloe came out to find them, a heavy, totally unsuitable perfume surrounding her. She was dressed up to the nines and grinning widely. 'I'm off then, Kristie. I'll see you in the morning. Bye, Radford. Have fun.'

'What did she mean, have fun?' asked Kristie sharply when she had gone. 'What were you two talking about before I came home?'

'Nothing.' Which was the truth, but for some reason Kristie didn't look as though she believed him. Not that he minded; he found it quite amusing. 'What could we talk about with Jake ever present? I quite like the suggestion, though.' He took her empty mug and placed it on the ground beside his own and then half turned towards her, reaching out to stroke a stray strand of hair from her cheek.

Her skin was soft and velvety and he allowed his fingers to linger for a moment longer than was necessary. She didn't move, only the slightly faster rise and fall of her breasts revealing her vulnerability. With greater daring he slid his hand beneath her chin and compelled her to face him. Her awesome green eyes were wide and troubled as if she knew she oughtn't to let him do this but for some reason she had no control.

He traced the pad of his thumb over her lips, feeling how

they trembled, feeling her breath warm on his palm. 'You're beautiful, Kristie, quite the most beautiful woman I've ever met.'

She edged back and her voice was husky. 'And there have been plenty?'

Did that bother her, the thought that he'd been out with other girls? He felt secret elation because it could mean only one thing. 'I've met plenty, yes, but there are not many that I've been serious about.'

'And you've never married?'

'I guess I haven't met the right girl.'

'Do you enjoy playing the field?'

'I don't play the field,' he told her sharply. Where had she got this impression?

'You mean you don't take a girl out, let her think you're serious about her, and then drop her when things start to get heavy?'

'Good lord, no. I would never do such a thing.'

'I'm not so sure,' she muttered.

Anger got the better of him. 'I don't know why you're so keen on making me out a blackguard,' he snorted. 'I can assure you that I'm nothing of the sort.' And if this conversation carried on the way it was going he would get precisely nowhere. Throwing caution to the winds, he took her face between his palms and kissed her. And even though she struggled he did not let her go.

The kiss thundered through his head, triggering responses in every corner of his body. His blood rushed out of control and his heart hammered non-stop. And even though there was no response from Kristie, even though she still fought him, he was determined to win. He knew that deep down inside she was feeling the same trembling emotions, but whereas he was giving them free rein Kristie was holding everything in check.

But she couldn't do it for ever.

Lord, she tasted beautiful—sweet and feminine and utterly sexy. His hormone levels rose by several hundred per cent and he couldn't contain a groan of desire. Still with his mouth pressed to hers, he slid an arm around her back and urged her to her feet so that he could hold her against him and feel the full impact of her sensational body.

It was almost his undoing. Only by sheer strength of will did he hold back. It was like being a teenager all over again. But twice as wonderful.

When Kristie's lips eventually parted on a sigh, allowing him to deepen the kiss, he knew he was on the verge of winning. And when her sigh was followed by a moan of sheer pleasure he felt triumphant.

She returned his kisses now with a hunger that amazed him. It was as though all her pent-up feelings had been released. Her tongue searched his mouth, tasting him as he had tasted her, her eyes closed, her hands roaming over his back, nails clutching. This was more than he'd expected and he took every possible advantage.

'Kristie—' he groaned against her mouth '—what are you doing to me?'

No answer, more moans, more kissing, more touching. He felt her breasts heaving against him and he knew that he had to touch them. Without either of them seeming to know what they were doing, he led her indoors. And there their lovemaking began in earnest.

All he had to do was run a finger over her sensationally pert nipples for her to jerk with pleasure. It pleased him that they were so sensitive and responsive, and in no time at all he had lifted off her silk top and flicked aside her lacy bra. His groin tightened and ached intolerably at the sight of all her beauty.

He stroked in wonder, gently at first but then hunger

getting the better of him. He cupped each breast and tweaked her nipples between finger and thumb, and her wild enjoyment only added to his own almost out of control desire. He laid her down on the couch and kneeling beside her he took each of her nipples in turn into his mouth. She squirmed and writhed and cried out, holding his head tightly as if wanting to keep him there for all time.

Allowing one hand to wander free, he touched and stroked, pushing her skirt aside in order to trace his fingers along the inside of her thighs. Higher and higher he went, each inch of the way expecting to be slapped back, but Kristie was beyond stopping him. She was thrashing about now, actually lifting herself so that he could find the moist, hot, heart of her. It was doing murderous things to him.

And he wanted more, but not here where Jake could wander down and find them. In her bedroom, with the door closed and no fear of being disturbed. 'Let's go to bed,' he whispered hoarsely, and she made no demur as he lifted her into his arms.

In fact she clung to him as he carried her upstairs, kissing him so fiercely and wildly that he almost fell. He felt as though he'd drunk a half bottle of whisky. Drunk on a woman's love! What a spectacular thought.

He hesitated at the top of the stairs. He saw Jake's door slightly ajar but which of the other three led to Kristie's room? She waved towards one of them and turned the handle as he nudged it open. Once inside he set her on her feet. A brief glance at the room showed that it was a little more personal than downstairs. A photograph on each of the bedside tables, a painting of an alleyway in some far off land on one of the walls, and a vase of silk flowers on the dressing table. But it was the bed that interested him most—a bed draped in cream satin. He couldn't wait to get her there.

It was with indecent haste that they undressed each other. She was so eager that it was hard to believe that she was the same person who had fended him off for so long. It made him wonder whether she had been like this with Jake's father. What a lucky man he had been, and what a fool for letting her down so badly.

Undoing the buttons on his shirt, Kristie kissed every inch of skin as it was exposed, doing to his nipples what he had done to her. It was an electrifying experience. And when she unbuckled his belt and slid down the zip on his trousers it took every ounce of his willpower not to throw her on the bed there and then and take what he wanted so badly.

He'd already kicked off his shoes and socks, and now all that remained were his briefs. Both of them stood for a few seconds facing each other, conscious that all that stood between them now were two tiny items of clothing. The last hurdle. Was she ready for it?

He thought so, but decided to lay her on the bed first. She was so gorgeously beautiful and sexy, the epitome of the perfect woman, that he wanted to feast his eyes on her for a few full minutes before they became one. Kristie, though, had other ideas. She was, amazingly, far more impatient and she grabbed at his navy briefs and began tugging them down.

'Two can play at that game,' he said with a grin and, tipping her on to the bed, he yanked off her panties and flung them into the air. They landed on one of the photos and, fearful it might get knocked over, he gently retrieved them, looking at the picture casually as he did so.

His heart slammed to a halt.

What the hell?

'Tarah!'

CHAPTER TWELVE

KRISTIE had forgotten in the heat of the moment about her sister's photograph. Now, with Radford gasping out Tarah's name, every little bit of desire fled. It brought back reality with a bang. What had she been thinking? She sat up and bunched her knees to her chin, watching the emotions that raced across his face.

He couldn't believe what he was seeing. He sat up and stared at the photo for a long frozen minute, and then slowly turned dark questioning eyes in her direction.

'Recognise her, do you?' she asked icily.

'What is—Tarah's—photograph doing—here?' he asked slowly and jerkily.

'Why, do you know her?' Kristie didn't want to admit at this stage that she knew all about the way he had treated her sister. She would save that pleasure for later.

'I—I used to go out with her.' And his eyes were drawn again to the picture in the plain silver frame.

Tarah was posed against a palm tree in some idyllic island paradise, pouting prettily for the camera. She had been so beautiful, with such a zest for life, that Kristie had to fight a lump in her throat. Life was so unfair. Be careful, she warned, don't give anything away yet. Radford still needs to suffer. 'Really? What happened between you?'

He slowly withdrew from the bed, standing a few feet away to look down at her. There was utter sadness on his face. 'We drifted apart. I guess it was never meant to be.'

Drifted apart? That was an understatement considering he was the one who had ended their relationship.

'But you haven't answered my question,' he said. 'Why have you got Tarah's photograph at your bedside?' And then he seemed to see her clearly for the very first time. He looked from her to the photograph and back again, shock and uncertainty in his eyes. 'You aren't—she's not—your sister?'

'She was.'

Radford frowned harshly. 'What do you mean, was?'

There was a long painful silence in the room before Kristie finally managed to choke out, 'She's dead.' And how she held back the tears she didn't know.

'She can't be.' The words were forced from a stiff throat. 'I haven't seen her for years, but—she can't be dead.'

'I can assure you she is,' snapped Kristie, glaring at him now. 'And I really don't wish to talk about it. Will you go?'

'But how—when—?'

'I've told you, it's too painful to talk about. Just leave me alone.'

He stepped into his trousers and pulled on his shirt. 'I don't understand.' Shoes and socks followed. 'You have to tell me, Kristie. I can't go away and—'

'Not now,' she insisted.

'Tomorrow, then. I'll come and see you in your office tomorrow.'

She supposed she owed him some sort of an explanation and tomorrow she wouldn't be feeling quite so emotional. Having virtually invited him into her bed hadn't helped. She felt stupid now. How could she have let herself get so carried away?

Because she couldn't help it, that was why. Because she was far too attracted to him for her own peace of mind.

Silently, he left the room, but Kristie didn't move until she heard his car start up and move away. She listened until she could no longer hear it and only then did she get up off the bed and drag her clothes back on.

In one way it was a relief he had found out. At the same time she wasn't yet ready to tell him about Jake. He hadn't suffered enough. Actually he hadn't suffered at all. And why should he be distressed about Tarah when he had lost all feelings for her? He would feel upset, yes, because he had once been close to her, but it wouldn't devastate him.

Kristie wasn't looking forward to their conversation the next day and when Chloe came home the first thing the girl saw was her unhappy face.

'What's happened?' she wanted to know. 'Didn't it go well with Radford?'

'What do you mean, go well? Did you two cook something up behind my back?' Have fun, Chloe had said, but Radford had denied knowing what she meant. Clearly, though, something had been said.

'Of course not,' insisted her house-mate. 'But I've seen the way he looks at you. And why did he turn up here if he didn't want to spend time with you? He's fallen for you, Kristie, in a big way.'

'You're talking rubbish,' Kristie defended. 'He wants an affair, I think, but he's not serious about me. He's never serious about any girl. And besides, I have Paul. He's asked me to marry him.'

'What?' The other girl's eyes were wide. 'You never said. When? Have you accepted? Gosh, this is exciting. I never thought he was serious about you, nor you him. I told Radford that—' She stopped short, her face flushing.

'You told Radford what—exactly?' asked Kristie. So she hadn't been wrong. And knowing that Chloe thought Radford the sexiest man on two legs, it wasn't difficult to guess what had been said.

'I mentioned that I thought Paul wasn't right for you, that's all.'

'And what gave you the right to say that?' asked Kristie crossly. 'You know nothing about my relationship with him. Paul's one of the kindest, most considerate men you could ever meet.'

'So why's it taken him this long to ask you to marry him?' questioned Chloe.

'Because he's not the sort to jump in with both feet.'

Chloe shook her head in disbelief. 'Or was it because you gave him the impression that you weren't in the market for marriage? But now that Radford's come on the scene he thought that he'd better make a move before he lost you altogether?'

Kristie hadn't realised how perceptive Chloe was, but she still intended to protect Paul. 'It's nothing of the sort. And I'm not happy with you discussing me behind my back.'

Chloe had the grace to look ashamed. 'So what did you say to Paul? Did you accept?'

'Not exactly. I'm thinking about it.'

'Which means,' said Chloe, 'that you don't really love him. Otherwise you'd have said yes straight away.'

'Jake needs a father.'

'And you think that marrying Paul is the answer? Don't do it, Kristie.'

'I would never marry Radford, if that's what you're thinking. Even if he asked me—which he never will.' It was the first time she'd had such a conversation with Chloe and she was not sure that it was wise. Chloe wasn't renowned for keeping her mouth shut. 'I think I'll go to bed,' she said now. 'Goodnight, Chloe. Oh, by the way, did you have a good night? I forgot to ask.'

'No, I didn't, as a matter of fact,' replied the other girl. 'My date didn't turn up. I went to the cinema on my own.'

'I'm sorry,' said Kristie.

Chloe shrugged her ample shoulders. 'It's the story of my life.'

Kristie couldn't sleep. Only a few hours ago she and Radford had lain here hot in the throes of passion. And if he hadn't seen her sister's photograph he would still be here. And they would have made love. And she would have enjoyed it—tremendously. She would have been drawn into his web of sex and excitement and she would have remained there until he decided he'd had enough of her.

She went cold at the very thought. What a merciful release she'd had. And all night long she endured the same recurring thoughts.

When morning came she was tempted to avoid him by working from home, except that she knew perfectly well that if she didn't turn up Radford would come looking for her. And it would be harder to get rid of him.

She'd been at her desk for about an hour before he paid her a visit; an hour in which she'd been unable to concentrate, flitting from one job to another, answering calls, making others, but wishing herself anywhere but here. She didn't want to talk about Tarah. She'd cried all her tears and put her heartache away and she didn't want to resurrect any of it.

'Good morning, Kristie. I've brought us some coffee and biscuits.'

Kristie let out a deep sigh. This had all the makings of a long visit and she wasn't up to it. She'd had all night to prepare herself and yet she still wasn't ready for this conversation.

'You didn't have to,' she said.

'But I wanted to.' He took the tray over to the two armchairs and indicated that he would like her to join him. 'You look tired. Didn't you sleep well?'

'Not really,' she admitted.

'I guess it was my fault for raking up the past. But you can't blame me. It was such a shock discovering that you're Tarah's sister. And then to be told that she's no longer alive. I find it hard to take in.'

'Not as much as I do,' she retorted, settling into her chair and deliberately staring out of the window rather than at him. His very presence sent her senses skittering and she knew that if she looked into his eyes she would be lost.

'Kristie, you don't have to bear this thing alone. It's sometimes best to talk.'

'You don't understand, do you?' She turned her head sharply and shot him a resentful glare, ignoring the way her pulses leapt. 'I don't want to talk. It's not something that happened recently. I've done all my grieving.'

'I still can't believe it,' he said, shaking his head. 'Tarah was always full of life. She had such great plans. How did it happen? When? I wasn't going to jump in with these questions straight away, but I can't help it. I've thought of nothing else all night long.'

He sounded as though he cared but she knew he didn't. His only concern was because Tarah was her sister and the shock of the discovery was ruining his plans to seduce her.

'And you think I haven't?' she snapped.

'I know you have,' he said quietly.

'If you knew that you'd do the decent thing and keep away.'

'I need to know what happened.'

'It was almost six years ago.' Her voice was so soft he had to lean forward to hear.

'That long?' he asked with a frown.

Kristie nodded. 'There was nothing the doctors could do for her.'

'Cancer?'

'No.'

'A road accident?'

'No, just a normal, routine operation.' If a Caesarean could be called normal. 'A woman's thing. Unfortunately complications set in. She never recovered.' She knew that by saying 'a woman's thing' she would stop him from asking any further questions.

He shook his head slowly, sitting right back in his chair, his fingers strumming the arms. 'It's unbelievable.'

'That's what I thought.'

'Do you have any other brothers or sisters? Tarah never talked about her family. I know she'd had an unhappy marriage, but that's as much as she told me.'

'There's no one else,' she said huskily.

'Parents?'

'Dead.'

He looked as though he didn't know where to put himself. 'So you're alone in the world?'

'I have Jake. He's my world.'

'I'd like to be a part of it too.' It was Radford's turn to speak quietly.

Kristie felt her heart give a leap, but she pretended not to hear and he didn't repeat it. Instead he passed her mug of coffee and offered the plate of biscuits. They were homemade and looked delicious but Kristie wasn't hungry even though she'd had no breakfast.

She sipped her drink and wished he would go. Of course he didn't. He sat there deep in thought, eating biscuit after biscuit until the plate was empty. He looked surprised to see them all gone.

'I have work to do,' said Kristie, getting to her feet.

'Can I take you out tonight?' he asked, rising too.

'I'm seeing Paul.'

'Tomorrow, then?'

'Isn't it time you went back to London?' she asked sharply. 'How can you afford to take so much time off?'

'I'm in touch every day. And at the moment I have something far more important to do.'

'Felicity's wedding is months away,' she retorted.

'I wasn't talking about Flick. Or my mother.'

Kristie's eyes flashed a brilliant green. 'If it's me, then you're wasting your time.' Despite her feelings, or even because of them, she was determined to keep her hatred well fuelled.

'Because of Paul?' he asked drily. 'I don't consider him a threat. In fact, I don't think you'll ever marry him.'

'Then you don't know me very well at all,' she riposted. Tonight she would accept Paul's proposal, and tomorrow she would wear his ring. And see what Radford had to say then.

CHAPTER THIRTEEN

RADFORD had been very fond of Tarah and he found it hard to accept that she was no longer alive. He had never met a girl so vivacious and full of fun and there had been times when he'd been close to asking her to marry him. He felt deeply saddened by the discovery and wished he had known at the time. No matter that they had parted on bad terms, he would have still paid his respects.

It was ironic that he'd now met her sister and had fallen deeply in love with her—a very different love from that he'd felt for Tarah. He couldn't help wondering what would have happened if Tarah was alive and he was still going out with her, and he then met Kristie. Maybe he would even have married Tarah. What sort of complications would have arisen then? He didn't dare think about it.

Kristie was the woman he had been waiting for all his life. A cliché, yes, but it was true. He'd fancied himself in love more than once, but always there had been a modicum of doubt at the back of his mind, something that stopped him from taking the final plunge. But with Kristie it was different. He wanted to spend the rest of his life with her. She had touched on the right nerve; she had taken his heart and made it her own. He was bound irrevocably to her.

The problem now was persuading her to feel the same about him. He had been boasting when he had said Paul wasn't a threat, but the way she had said, 'Then you don't know me very well at all' troubled him deeply. It sounded as though she had definitely made up her mind to marry him. And if that was the case he needed to do something about it quickly.

'I think I know you better than you realise,' he said. 'If you're going to marry Paul simply to spite me then it will be the biggest mistake of your life. And I would urge you not to do it.'

Her eyes flashed in that beautiful way that sent his testosterone levels rising. 'So that you think you'd stand a better chance?'

'Not at all. And I really mean that. Whether our relationship develops or not, I don't want you doing something that you'll later regret.' He did wonder whether Kristie knew who he was, whether she knew that he'd been dating her sister. But even so he couldn't see that as a reason for her disliking him. The culprit here was definitely Jake's father.

She still looked at him suspiciously. 'Why?'

'Because I care for you. Whether you believe that or not I don't know.'

'I don't,' she answered sharply.

He winced. It seemed there was nothing he could say or do that would change her mind about him. But he would never give up. It was time he left her now, though. Kristie was already moving back to her desk.

'Maybe I'll see you later?' he asked as he reached the door.

'Maybe,' she agreed, but not with much enthusiasm.

'And I really am sorry about Tarah. You have my deepest sympathy.'

She didn't look at him again, her eyes were already on the papers in front of her. He closed the door quietly.

'Come in, Paul.' Kristie had invited Paul to supper and her nerves were a bit jittery.

She had thought long and hard about whether to accept

his proposal, and yet really there had been nothing to think about. She couldn't marry him; it was as simple as that.

'I can't keep you in suspense,' she said, as soon as they had walked through to her living room and sat down with a drink. 'I was going to wait until later in the evening but it wouldn't be fair.'

He looked into her sad green eyes. 'I think I know what you're going to say.'

'I'm sorry, Paul.' She gave a wistful smile. 'It wouldn't work. I love you dearly as a friend and I've tried to feel something more for you, you've no idea how much I've tried, but I simply can't. I know Jake adores you, but marrying you for Jake's sake is not the answer. And keeping you hanging on isn't the answer either. I should never have done it.'

He looked crushed and she wanted to hug him, but it would be too dangerous. She might say the wrong thing out of pity. 'It's Radford, isn't it?' he asked quietly, his fingers clenching around his glass. 'You've fallen for him?'

Kristie nodded and looked down at an invisible spot on the carpet. 'I didn't want to. I can't even think how it happened because—'

'Never mind how it happened,' he cut in. 'I think I knew the first time I saw him that he was a rival, no matter how much you denied it. He has far more going for him than I have.'

'It isn't his money,' declared Kristie. 'And in truth I'm annoyed with myself for feeling anything. I've fought it ever since I met him.'

'Why? Because of me?'

Kristie gave a weak smile and nodded. It wouldn't hurt to let Paul think that.

'Actually, I think I already knew what your answer

would be,' he admitted. 'I hoped you'd agree to marry me, of course I did, but deep down inside I knew I was clutching at straws. You've always been totally honest with me.'

'I'm sorry,' she whispered, putting her hand over his.

He put his over the top of it and they were quiet for a moment. 'This is the end, isn't it?' he asked.

Kristie nodded.

He took a long swallow of his beer. 'I guess I need to get on with my life, find myself another girl, and try to forget you. Not that I ever will—forget you, I mean. You're a sweet, kind girl, Kristie. Whether you marry Radford or whether you marry someone else, he'll be the luckiest man alive.' He was silent for a moment before saying, 'Do you mind if I don't stay for supper?'

The lump in Kristie's throat was hard to swallow and she shook her head. 'I truly am sorry, Paul.'

'Me, too,' he admitted with a nod. 'I'll see myself out.'

Kristie felt truly awful after he'd gone, and she threw their supper into the bin because she couldn't face eating. This was the worst thing she'd ever had to do but she'd made the right decision, of that she was sure. It would have been so unfair on Paul to keep him hanging on any longer. In one way she had Radford to thank for bringing it to a head.

Her sleep was disturbed that night and it was something of a relief when she discovered the next day that Radford had been called back to London. Hopefully he would stay there for a long time.

'He was reluctant to go,' Felicity told Kristie when she arrived at the office next. 'Would it have something to do with you? He looked sort of sad.'

'Who knows?' said Kristie with a shrug.

'Have you told him there's absolutely no hope?'

'Constantly.'

'So it's nothing new?'

'Maybe he finally got the message,' she suggested, while knowing that nothing was further from the truth. He'd turn up again, if only to find out whether she was marrying Paul.

'My mother wants to know whether you'd like to join us for dinner tonight.'

Kristie frowned. 'Is it a special occasion?'

'No, she simply thought it would be nice for us to meet socially instead of always talking business.'

She couldn't help wondering if there was any significance in her asking while Radford was absent. Did Peggy want to quiz her about him? Felicity had said that she'd seen her mother watching them when they were together. She'd said she thought it was why she had offered her the use of an office and that she'd never cared for his previous choice of girlfriends.

The whole thing sounded ominous, yet what excuse had she? Chloe would be at home so there was nothing to worry about where Jake was concerned. So reluctantly she accepted. 'Tell her I'd love to. I can be here about eight. I have to bathe Jake and put him to bed first.'

'Yes,' Felicity said with interest. 'Radford told us about your son and the mistake he'd made thinking he belonged to your lodger.'

'Not my lodger,' Kristie corrected, 'my general factotum. She does anything and everything. I wouldn't be without her.'

'So, if it's not a rude question, where's the boy's father?' asked Felicity. Then she saw the murderous expression that crossed Kristie's face and added quickly, 'I'm sorry. I shouldn't have asked that. It's none of my business. I'll tell my mother you've accepted.' And with that she wheeled away.

Kristie spent the rest of the day wondering whether she'd

done the right thing in accepting Peggy's invitation. But what was done was done; she couldn't change it. And knowing that Radford would be absent helped; it helped her get through the day too. She was able to concentrate more fully on the work in hand. This was how it should be, how it had been before she met him.

It seemed a different world that she lived in now. A world where her senses were being taken over by a man she desperately wanted to despise. They were scary feelings and always she banished them, but they had a way of wriggling themselves back to the surface. Perhaps the whole truth of the matter was that she was afraid to let herself get too closely involved in case he rejected her the same way as he had Tarah. He was such an easy man to like, to love. To *what*? How had love come into the equation?

Kristie shook her head, buried the thought, and got on with her work. And every time it threatened to raise its head again she battered it back down. She didn't even want to think along those lines. Of course she didn't love him.

It was almost time for her to go when she had a phone call from Radford. She'd picked it up and answered cheerfully, 'A Day to Remember, Kristie Swift speaking.'

'Hello, Kristie Swift,' he said, and much to her annoyance the sound of his voice set her pulses racing. She'd convinced herself that it was nothing like love that she felt—it was a physical thing, some sort of chemical reaction over which she had no control. And she was determined to fight it. She put the tips of her fingers to the pulse at the base of her throat and felt it leaping. Damn him! How could he do this to her?

'You sound happy today,' he said. 'Would that be because you've finally agreed to marry the man you don't love, or because you've rejected him and it's a great load off your mind?'

Kristie closed her eyes, picturing him gloating, and a swift feeling of anger came over her. 'It's none of your business,' she snapped.

'Oh, I think it's very much my business. You could not possibly respond to me the way you do if you were in love with another man. Therefore you don't love him. Therefore you've told him so. I hope. Am I right?'

'I don't have to answer. If that's all you've phoned me for then you're wasting your time.'

'I don't think so. The fact that you're not telling me is answer enough,' he said with a smile in his voice. 'If you had agreed to marry Paul you'd have been quick to ram it down my throat. Congratulations, Kristie—you've done the right thing.'

'Damn you!' she spat.

Another smile from him—a triumphant smile. She could see it in her mind's eye. He would consider her fair game now. Her life would be sheer hell. Unless she succumbed, of course. And it would be so easy to do that. Even thinking about it sent a trail of destruction through her body. 'It's time for me to go home,' she said tersely. 'Is that all you've phoned me for?'

'What are you thinking, Kristie?' he asked in a low, seductive voice. 'You sound panic stricken. Are you afraid that you might do the unthinkable and let yourself actually like me?'

'Never!'

'Never is a long time. And we've already got through one barrier.'

'Which I deeply regret,' she riposted. 'There certainly won't be a repeat.'

'Mm, I wonder.'

The way he said it, suggesting that he'd enjoy trying and would undoubtedly find her easy prey, created further unwanted sensations. Because she knew beyond any shadow of doubt that she would be unable to resist him if he made a full-scale attack on her senses. Radford Smythe *was* irresistible. There, she'd admitted it. She'd fallen for him.

Heaven help her.

'I hear my mother's invited you to dinner tonight. It's a pity I won't be there.'

'Maybe that's the very reason she invited me,' suggested Kristie. 'Maybe she knows that I don't like you.'

'My mother thinks everyone should fall in love with me. I'm her blue-eyed boy, didn't you know that?'

Kristie gave a mirthless laugh. 'It's natural she'd have a biased view—mothers always do.' She did herself. She thought Jake was the most gorgeous, intelligent little boy there ever was. There was no one to beat him. It didn't matter that he was adopted; she loved him as if he were her own child.

'I'll be back by the weekend. Enjoy yourself tonight.'

'I'll do my best.'

'I'll be thinking of you,' he added on a soft growl.

And she would be thinking what a relief it was that he wasn't joining them. Except that the conversation would be sure to touch on him. There would really be no escape. His presence would be felt whether he was there or not. She slammed down the phone and was fuming as she walked to the car. She really ought not to have accepted Peggy's invitation.

Normally, when she was driving, she kept her mobile phone switched on in case Chloe needed to get in touch with her. But she was so disturbed by her conversation with Radford that she forgot. When she arrived home she found an empty house—and a hastily scribbled note from Chloe

to say that Jake had had an accident and been taken to
hospital.

Kristie's heart panicked as she raced back to her car.
What kind of an accident? Oh, God, please, please, don't
let anything happen to him, she prayed.

CHAPTER FOURTEEN

RADFORD felt pleased after he had finished talking to Kristie. She wasn't going to marry Paul after all. He felt on top of the world, fairly dancing around his London apartment. She might still try to keep her distance but there was hope now where there had been none before.

Later he was having dinner with a client but for the moment he could devote all his thoughts to the woman he loved. He only had to think about her to feel an arousal. Especially when he pictured her stunning naked body. She was incredibly beautiful—so slender, so perfectly formed, with skin as soft as thistledown. If it hadn't been for that photograph of Tarah he would have made love to her. It would, he felt, have been a turning point in their relationship.

He wondered then, as he had at the time, whether Kristie knew who he was. There had been an odd inflection in her voice when she'd asked him whether he recognised Tarah. And if she did know why hadn't she mentioned it?

When he took his shower later he was still thinking about her. It would give him a great deal of pleasure to melt her resistance. He was looking forward to it immensely.

A little red light blinked at him from the telephone, telling him he had missed a call. Perhaps tonight's engagement was off? He wouldn't mind because he could sit here thinking about Kristie, planning how he would woo her. The mere thought of it gave him immense pleasure.

He pressed the button. 'Radford, pick up the phone.' It was his mother, impatient as usual to speak with him, hating having to talk to a machine. 'I've just had a call from Chloe, Kristie's friend. Jake's in hospital. I thought you'd want to know.'

His heart leapt into his throat and he immediately phoned his mother back. But she couldn't tell him anything more. 'Something about an accident. I don't know exactly. But if I hear anything I'll—'

'I'm on my way,' cut in Radford at once. 'Kristie will need someone with her. Which hospital is it?'

Kristie was out of her mind with worry. Jake was in surgery and there was nothing she could do but wait. Chloe was in floods of tears. 'It's all my fault,' she kept saying. 'I'll never forgive myself, never.'

When Kristie arrived at the hospital it had taken her ages to get any sense out of Chloe. The girl kept sobbing uncontrollably, beside herself with worry and guilt and Kristie had to shout at her to make her stop and tell her what had happened.

'I picked Jake up from school as usual,' she said tremulously. 'We were almost home when he saw the Browns' new little puppy in their garden. He let go my hand and raced across the road before I could stop him. He didn't even look.'

There were more sobs before she could go on.

'I saw the car and I yelled at Jake, but it was too late. The driver didn't stand a chance of stopping. Jake looked like a rag doll as he was flung in the air.' Chloe buried her face in her hands, her shoulders heaving as she relived that fateful moment. 'He didn't move. I was so scared—I thought he was dead.' She couldn't go on then, her throat was choked with emotion and the tears wouldn't stop. 'Oh, God, Kristie, what have I done? I am so sorry.'

Tears streamed down Kristie's cheeks too but she tried

to be strong for Chloe's sake. 'Don't blame yourself. It could have happened to me.' Jake adored the little dog and at times like that, no matter how often he'd been told not to run across the road without checking for traffic, he would forget. All he'd be interested in was the puppy.

Suddenly she remembered that she was supposed to be dining at the Mandervell-Smythes' and she gave Chloe the task of phoning Peggy and explaining. It was something for the girl to do and for a few minutes took her mind off the terror of what had happened. Nevertheless they were both still clinging to each other and crying when one of the doctors came to find them. He smiled reassuringly. 'Which one of you is Jake's mother?'

'I am,' answered Kristie, standing up. 'How is he?'

'We've just finished operating. You have nothing to worry about—he'll pull through.'

He would never know what a relief it was to hear him say that. Kristie felt like kissing him. 'Is he badly hurt?' Chloe had been unable to tell her anything.

'He's very bruised, naturally, and he has a broken arm, but he also ruptured his spleen, which was our main concern. He lost a lot of blood and he'll need a top up, but other than that he'll do fine. He's a very lucky young boy. I suggest you both go and have a cup of tea.'

'Can I see him?' A drink was the furthest thought from her mind.

'As soon as we get him settled in ITU. I'll come and find you myself.' He laid a reassuring hand on Kristie's shoulder. 'No more tears now.'

She smiled weakly and thanked him, and she and Chloe headed for the cafeteria. The coffee was strong and bitter and, although she was still desperately worried it stopped her from shaking.

The tears started again though when she saw Jake. He

was asleep, so still and pale and tiny and vulnerable, that it was all she could do not to throw herself down beside him and hug him and hug him and will some of her strength into him. Thank God he was alive. She'd had all sorts of visions as she had raced to the hospital, even while she'd sat waiting for news. In fact, the relief of seeing him made her legs buckle and Chloe was the one to slide her a chair.

She lost track of time as she sat at his bedside holding his hand, stroking his brow, trying to ignore all the tubes that were fixed to his tiny body. He was constantly monitored and checked and every time the nurse came Kristie asked if he was all right and was reassured that everything was as it should be.

Kristie sent Chloe home. There was nothing she could do and Kristie had listened to enough apologies. It was while she was whispering to Jake that she loved him and would he please hurry and wake up so that she could talk to him that she felt a hand on her shoulder.

Looking up, she saw Radford and for the first time ever she was pleased to see him. He was someone solid she could depend on. She stood up and, as his arms came about her, she buried her head in his shoulder, tears flowing again, but tears of relief this time. She didn't have to bear this alone.

Radford pulled up a chair and sat beside Kristie, holding her hand, murmuring soothing words, not really knowing what he was saying, or even caring. His main concern was Kristie. He'd stood a few moments watching her before he had made his presence known and his heart had gone out to her. She'd looked so fragile, so afraid, willing her life into this battered little boy.

Daylight was filtering into the room when Jake woke. They had both sat watching him for a very long time, talking quietly. Kristie had explained what had happened and he'd expressed his concern. And all the time Jake lay there pale and lifeless, only the machine that monitored him telling them that he was alive.

Then the boy's eyes slowly opened. 'Mummy,' he whispered.

'Darling.' Mindful of his injuries, Kristie carefully hugged him.

'I love you, Mummy.'

'I love you too, sweetheart.'

'I'm tired.' And he drifted back to sleep.

'He's going to be all right,' she said with a relieved smile.

Radford nodded. 'And now that you know, don't you think you ought to go home and get some sleep yourself?'

Kristie shook her head very definitely. 'Not until he's properly awake and I know for certain.'

'So let's go and get some coffee.' She looked desperately tired and very pale too. He took her arm as she got to her feet and he didn't let it go as they walked to the cafeteria. It wasn't yet open but there was a hot drinks machine nearby and they sat on the corridor chairs with their plastic cups cradled in their hands.

'How did you know about Jake?' asked Kristie.

'My mother phoned and told me.'

'And you drove all the way from London just to be with me?'

He nodded. 'It was the least I could do. I couldn't let you suffer alone. I bet Chloe's not feeling too happy?' He didn't tell her that he'd nearly had an accident too. In his desperation to be with her he'd been driving far too fast, had only come to his senses when he'd almost hit a car that had swerved in front of him on the motorway.

'She can't stop apologising. It's why I sent her home. It's not her fault. Kids will be kids.'

'That's very magnanimous of you. Are you sure she deserves it?' If it had been his child he'd have throttled the woman.

'So long as Jake's OK I can't really lay the blame on her.'

'And you'll carry on employing her?'

'Of course. Jake loves her. The ideal solution would be for me to give up work myself and look after Jake full time, but needs must. I can't live on fresh air.'

'If you married me you wouldn't need to work again.' Dammit, he hadn't meant to say that. Not in this place, not at this time. What the hell was he thinking of? He felt her go tense beside him. 'I'm sorry. That was uncalled for. Forget I said it.' But he wouldn't forget. He would say it again one day, when Jake was better, when he felt the time was right.

'Let's go and see if Jake's awake,' she said quietly.

A nurse stood by the bed, checking the blood that was steadily dripping into Jake, and she smiled as they approached. 'Your little man's fully awake, dying to see his mummy and daddy.'

'I'm not the father,' said Radford.

'Oh, well, whoever you are I'm sure he'll be pleased to see you,' responded the nurse cheerfully. 'He's doing well.'

Radford smiled as he watched Kristie give her son a big kiss. The bond between them was unmistakable. Such tenderness, such love. Would he ever experience that? He turned his head away, feeling an unexpected lump in his throat. The nurse had gone and he busied himself looking at all the equipment, giving Kristie a moment or two alone with her son. The label on the blood caught his attention and for a second it surprised him. AB negative. Very rare.

He was AB positive himself and he understood that two positives made a negative. He looked at Kristie. 'Your blood group must be rare too. Something else we have in common.'

She glanced at him and shook her head and turned her attention quickly back to Jake.

He frowned. Something didn't add up here. 'What are you saying?'

This time when she glanced at him there was a haunted expression in her eyes and a look of guilt on her face and for a moment he couldn't understand what was wrong. Then he looked at Jake—and he saw what he should have seen clearly before. He saw Tarah, not Kristie.

He looked at Kristie again and there was nothing of Jake in her. Could this, therefore, be Tarah's child and Kristie had taken him in when her sister had died? And if that was the case, who was the father? Did it, could it, be *his* son? His heart leapt into his throat. No, no, it had to be some other man's. Tarah hadn't been pregnant when their affair had ended. But the blood groups? Was it too much of a coincidence? The time span was right. Perhaps she had been pregnant and hadn't told him. And Kristie's stricken expression suddenly said it all.

She had been watching him, seeing the thoughts flood through his mind, seeing realisation dawn, and she turned away with a cry of despair.

But he said nothing in front of Jake. He waited until the boy had drifted to sleep again then he took Kristie outside into the corridor. 'You and I have to talk,' he said grimly. 'Jake's my son, isn't he?'

Kristie looked anywhere but into his eyes and he took her by the shoulders and forced her to face him. 'Isn't he?'

She nodded uncomfortably.

His suspicions confirmed, Radford felt a most peculiar

pang in his stomach. He couldn't even begin to describe it. He let her go and turned away, then he turned back again just as quickly. 'My son!' he rasped. 'And you never told me. God in heaven, woman, why?'

He was disappointed in her. She had shattered both his trust and the love that had been growing inside him. Tarah had let him down, and now Kristie too. What had she hoped to gain from it? He couldn't begin to understand her reasoning. She hadn't even let on that she knew who he was. Why?

Because she'd wanted to keep Jake to herself, that was why. She was one of those possessive women who couldn't bear to share. Like Tarah! Tarah had been possessive. She had hated it when he had so much as looked at another girl. He felt truly crushed.

'Why, Kristie?' He needed to hear it from her own lips.

'Because he's mine now,' she shrieked, becoming suddenly furiously alive. 'I adopted him. He's nothing to do with you.' He had never seen her so incensed. Her eyes had darkened dramatically and were fiercely beautiful.

'How can you say that?' His thick brows beetled across his forehead. 'He's very much my son, and I think the law would agree with me.' He wanted Jake—he wanted him with a passion that surprised him. From being a man who couldn't care less about children he had become an enraged father all in one fell swoop. This was his own flesh and blood and belonged with him. Kristie could go to hell.

'It was the law who let me adopt him,' she pointed out. 'He's been mine since he was a few hours old, and if you think you're going to—'

'What do you mean, a few hours?' he cut in, feeling a cold chill steal down his spine.

'Tarah died shortly after he was born. She never even

got to hold him. So he's mine, and I shall see to it that you never get your hands on him.'

This was getting out of control, and a hospital corridor was no place to argue. He needed time to think. 'I'm going home to get washed and changed,' he said. 'I suggest you do the same. I'll speak to you again later.'

Outside the hospital Radford took several deep, steadying breaths. His whole world had been turned upside down in a matter of minutes. He was a father. Jake was his son. It was beyond comprehension. He wondered whether Kristie would ever have told him. He was disappointed in her, deeply disappointed. How could she have been so cruel?

It was hard to believe that all along she had known who he was, and yet he still couldn't understand why she hated him so much. Or perhaps it wasn't hatred—perhaps it was because she had thought he would take Jake off her if he ever found out, and so she'd tried to keep him at arm's length. What she hadn't taken into account was the fact that she might be attracted to him. She could deny it as much as she liked but her body told a different story. And he didn't think it was pure lust because Kristie didn't strike him as being that type of person.

But this had nothing to do with their current dilemma. She had let him down. He was hurt that she had kept the knowledge to herself. They were two for a pair, these sisters. Tarah had shattered his trust all those years ago and Kristie had done the same now. Dammit, why did he always fall for the wrong type? Why couldn't he see through them? Was he doomed never to get married?

But the fact was that he now had a son and he intended to fight Kristie tooth and nail for custody of him. To hell with the fact that she'd adopted him—there had to be a way round it.

When he got home he told his concerned mother about Jake's injuries, but not about his discovery. That could wait. He had a lot of thinking to do first.

Kristie didn't go home; she stayed with Jake. She was petrified now that she would lose him. Her worst nightmare was being realised. The law would be on Radford's side, he'd said. Would it? Could he take Jake off her? She didn't know and her ignorance was her biggest fear.

Chloe came back and when she saw Kristie's pale, strained face she insisted that she go home and get some rest. 'I'll sit with Jake. I won't let anything else happen to him, I promise.'

Kristie reluctantly agreed. She'd had no sleep for twenty-four hours and was on the verge of collapse. Coupled with Radford finding out about Jake, she felt drained of every possible emotion. But what if he came back while she was absent? What if he'd already set the law into motion? Her mind spun out of control. She heard Chloe cry out, felt her legs give way, and the next thing she knew she was sitting in a chair and a nurse was offering her a glass of water.

'What happened?' she croaked as she took a sip of the cool liquid.

'You fainted. You haven't eaten or slept for the last twenty-four hours. You must go home now and go to bed.'

'But Jake,' she protested. She was scared of leaving him.

'Jake will be all right. He's having the very best of attention.'

'You won't leave him alone?' They didn't know that Radford might come along and kidnap him. And she was being fanciful. He couldn't do anything while Jake was in this state.

The nurse smiled. 'Of course we won't leave him. Besides, your friend's here. Your son likes Chloe, doesn't he?

And there's your boyfriend as well. I expect he'll be back soon.'

Kristie closed her eyes. Boyfriend! Enemy would be more like it. She didn't want him anywhere near Jake. And yet how could she stop him? He had as much right as she had. Possibly more. It hurt her to even think that, but Jake was his flesh and blood after all.

Chloe said now, 'You don't look fit to drive, Kristie. I'll run you home and then come straight back.'

'No!' She almost screeched the word, and both Chloe and the nurse looked at her in surprise. 'I can drive myself. I'll be OK. I want you to stay with Jake. He'll be scared when he wakes up if neither of us are here.'

She saw the nurse look at Chloe over the top of her head and lift her brows. They clearly both thought she was being neurotic, which she probably was. But with just cause. She finished the water and stood up. She felt slightly unsteady but not enough to stop her walking out of the hospital and driving home. 'I'll see you in a few hours, Chloe,' she said. 'Keep a close watch on Jake and ring me if there's a problem, anything at all.'

'There won't be,' Chloe assured her, but Kristie knew better. There was one very big problem—and his name was Radford Smythe.

Radford woke with a much clearer head. He'd sat up for hours thinking about Jake before finally falling asleep, but now he had everything sorted in his mind.

Discovering that he had a son had been the biggest shock of his life; more so than when he'd found out that Tarah was dead. And he couldn't think how it had happened because he and Tarah had always taken the utmost care. Besides, he'd never wanted children—he'd seen enough of his cousin's two unruly boys to put him off them for life.

But then he'd met Jake, and a more well-behaved or better mannered boy he couldn't have wished to meet. It made him think that maybe it wouldn't be so bad to be a father after all. Perhaps with Kristie as the mother? What a thought that had been. He'd imagined himself marrying her and them having either a brother or sister for Jake.

It had been nothing short of miraculous discovering that Jake was his own flesh and blood. The feelings it evoked were impossible to put into words. He felt—what did he feel? Amazed, for one thing—truly amazed. Exhilarated as well. He had created another human being—a living, loving human being. But also he was angry that he hadn't been told. He could have gone his whole life and never found out. It didn't bear thinking about.

But he was no longer angry with Kristie. She had done what she had thought best. Had she been a scheming woman, which was his first harsh thought, she would have hit him for a financial contribution to Jake's upbringing years ago. As it was, she had struggled to bring him up alone—and had done a very good job of it. Now it was up to him to help her.

And the best solution all round, as far as he could see, was to marry Kristie. That way they would both be happy. The three of them would be happy. Jake would have a father as well as a mother and the family would be complete.

It might take a little while for her to agree to his offer, but even she would surely see that it was by far the best solution. There would be no heartache for either of them. He couldn't wait to put his proposition to her.

But on his arrival at the hospital he found only Chloe. 'Kristie's gone home,' she said. 'She fainted and the nurse insisted she go and get something to eat and then try to sleep.'

Radford's first instinct was to go to her, but he made himself stay and chat to Chloe and Jake for a few minutes. Jake, he was pleased to see, was looking much better. He had colour in his cheeks now and it made Radford's heart swell to look at him and realise that this was his very own son. He wanted to tell Jake, but this wasn't the moment. Soon he would, though; soon they would be a proper father and son. He couldn't wait for that moment.

'I'll go and see how Kristie is,' he said after a while.

'Maybe you ought to take my key,' volunteered Chloe, 'in case she's asleep. It wouldn't be right to wake her. She was so exhausted when she left here.'

He smiled. 'A good idea.' In more ways than one. There was always the chance that Kristie wouldn't let him in, especially after the way he'd threatened her with the law. He was sorry for that now. It had been a heat of the moment thing. He hadn't been able to understand why she hadn't told him and his blood had boiled.

He knocked softly on the door when he arrived at the house but there was no answer and so he turned the key in the lock and walked in. Kristie was nowhere to be seen. He looked through the kitchen window into the garden but she wasn't there either. He called her name and slowly began to mount the stairs, but before he reached the top she appeared before him. She still had the same clothes on as before and she stood staring down at him, arms akimbo, face furious. 'What are you doing here? How did you get in?'

'Chloe lent me her key. I didn't want to bang on the door and wake you.'

'If you thought I might be asleep why did you come?' she retorted. 'You have no right creeping into my house and—'

'I was concerned about you. Chloe said that you'd fainted

and I wanted to make sure you were all right.' He climbed the last steps and halted in front of her. She looked so tired and pale and worried that he wanted to hold her tight and assure her that everything was going to be all right.

'You mean that you've come to tell me you're claiming Jake,' she yelled, her eyes over-bright, her cheeks suddenly flaming. 'Over my dead body. Jake's mine and he's staying mine.'

'Kristie, I'm not going to take him away from you,' he said gently.

'You're not?' She looked surprised. 'Then why—'

'Am I here?' he cut in. 'Because I have the perfect solution. But first of all I want to apologise for the way I spoke to you. I was totally out of order. You've no idea how much of a shock it was to discover that Jake is my son. And when that had sunk in all I wanted was to claim him as mine.'

She looked briefly ashamed.

'But then I realised that it wouldn't be fair on you. You've treated him as your own all these years. You've grown to love him and—'

'He is mine,' she maintained. 'In every sense of the word.'

'I realise that's how you must think, but listen to it from my side. Jake is my flesh and blood. He is my son, whichever way you look at it.' He saw the panic begin to rise. 'And no, I am not going to take him off you; I have a much better idea. And not one that's new to me either. I want you to marry me, Kristie.'

CHAPTER FIFTEEN

RADFORD waited with bated breath for Kristie's answer. To him, getting married was the perfect solution—the only solution. They were compatible in so many ways. And now that she knew she needn't fear that he would take Jake off her, what other reason would she have for saying no?

And yet she did say it. And she didn't mince her words. 'If you think I'd marry a man like you then you don't know yourself very well,' she stormed. 'Just look at the way you treated my sister. Do you really think I'd put myself in the same position? I know what would happen if we did get married. Give it a few months and you'd chuck me out on the dirt pile the same way as you did Tarah—then you'd claim Jake as your own.'

Radford was aghast by Kristie's outburst. He hadn't a clue what she was talking about. What had Tarah said to make Kristie feel like this? 'What are you suggesting?' he asked, a deep frown darkening his brow. 'I didn't—'

'No, of course you didn't do anything, did you?' she cut in furiously. 'You didn't end your relationship simply because you thought she was getting too serious, did you? You didn't end it because you were scared she wanted a family? Oh, no, you wouldn't admit to that.' She was fairly bouncing on her feet now. 'And now that you've discovered you do have a child, then you want him, and you're prepared to go to any lengths to get him. How two-faced is that? Damn you, Radford. Damn you to hell.'

There was something seriously wrong here and he intended to get to the bottom of it. 'Are you suggesting that Tarah told you I was the one to end our relationship?'

'I am.' She folded her arms across her chest and looked at him haughtily. 'She was distraught.'

'Tarah lied.' He tried to keep calm but in reality he was raging inside and he knew it wouldn't be long before he let it all out.

'Oh, you'd say that, wouldn't you,' she snapped. 'Now that she's no longer here to defend herself. What a coward you are. Why won't you admit the truth?'

'It is the truth,' he bellowed, his patience finally running out. 'Tarah was the one to put an end to things. As a matter of fact, she was never the perfect sister that you seem to think. I could tell you a hundred and one things she had wrong with her, but you wouldn't believe me, would you? Blood's thicker than water and all that.' Tarah had been jealous and possessive, but despite that he had loved her and had thought she had loved him. It had come as a shock when she had finished with him.

'And you're Mr Perfect, are you?' Kristie spat, her eyes over-bright, her whole body shaking with rage. 'You killed my sister, do you realise that? If you hadn't got her pregnant she'd never have died. I hate you from the bottom of my heart. Go, now, because I'm very tempted to push you down the stairs and put an end to your life too.'

So this was the reason she had been so hostile towards him. Poor Kristie, how she had suffered. But he knew that nothing he could say at this moment would help matters. 'Maybe I should go.' He breathed in deeply through his nose, his chest rising, his eyes never leaving hers. 'But this isn't the end of our conversation. I still think that getting married is the wisest decision. I'll leave you to think about it. It's either me and Jake, or nothing at all.'

*   *   *

Kristie watched Radford going back down the stairs—she watched with hatred in her eyes and dread in her heart. Not only had she got a sick son to worry about, but the very real fear that she would have him taken off her.

And what was that Radford had said about Tarah dumping him? He had to be lying; he simply did. Tarah wouldn't have told her own sister an untruth; she'd have no reason to. She'd been heartbroken when she had phoned and said that Radford had finished with her. There'd have been no tears if she'd been the one to end their relationship.

But she hadn't got time to think about this now. She must go back to the hospital—Jake would be asking for her. She hadn't slept much—a few short minutes at a time, that was all. It was impossible.

Downstairs she found Chloe's key on the hall table and she slipped it into her pocket. At least it meant that he couldn't sneak up on her again. She'd been scared half to death when she had heard him climbing the stairs; she'd thought it was a burglar, that perhaps in her distress she'd left the front door open.

And as for his suggestion that they get married—was he insane? They both knew his only reason was so that he could get hold of Jake. Kristie didn't take into account the fact that he'd asked her once before; that went completely out of her mind. All she knew was that he wanted Jake and that he'd go to any lengths to get him.

She spent the rest of the day at the hospital, fearful that Radford might put in a further appearance, mightily relieved when he didn't. And that evening she went home with Chloe. She wanted to stay, desperately. She was so afraid of what Radford might do, but in reality she knew that he couldn't do very much, not with Jake attached to so many machines. It would be inhuman to take him away.

Jake wanted Flopsy, his bunny rabbit. It was a soft toy

he'd long outgrown but he wanted it now. Kristie had stored it in the loft with a lot of other toys he no longer used, and it was while she was looking for it that she came upon a box she'd brought back from her sister's flat in London. It contained personal items that she'd not had the heart to look at at the time and she'd forgotten all about them. Now, she decided, might be a good idea to go through them.

But it was long after Chloe had gone to bed before she felt able to do so. Memories had resurrected themselves today. Her conversation with Radford had upset her and she'd said things she didn't mean, like wanting to push him down the stairs. When she said it she had meant it, but not now. He hadn't known Tarah was pregnant when they split up. She couldn't, in all honesty, lay the blame on him. Even though she had done so all these years.

So what had caused her change of heart? Was it because she had fallen in love with him? Because she had, there was no doubt about it. It wasn't something that she'd wanted to happen—the feelings had crept up on her unawares and, if she was honest with herself, she would rather she didn't feel anything. It would make things so much easier if she still hated him—because she felt very sure that she was going to have a fight on her hands where Jake was concerned.

She went cold all over every time she thought about Jake and the near miss he'd had. He could so easily have been killed. Her whole life would have been ruined because he *was* her life.

When she finally opened the box the first thing Kristie picked up was a photograph of Tarah and Radford. They were both laughing, having clearly set the camera to take the picture automatically. Kristie had done that with herself and Jake many times and it was always a mad scramble to get into position in time.

Tarah looked so happy, her head resting on Radford's shoulder, his arm around her. They were a perfect couple and Kristie found it hard to believe that Tarah would have ended their relationship. Why had she done that? Why would she have lied? What had really happened? Would she ever find out?

There were more photographs, some of Tarah on her own, posing, pouting, flirting, being typically outrageous Tarah, and some taken again with Radford. A few were of Radford on his own. Kristie studied these, wondering what the odds were against her meeting the man who had been her sister's lover. A man who lived over a hundred miles away. And, what was more amazing, she had fallen in love with him.

It was a preposterous thought, one that had dawned on her slowly over the last few days. He aroused her sexually, yes, but that was all, she had kept telling herself. She didn't like him in any other sense. They'd done nothing but fight since they'd met. How could it be love?

She tucked the thought away and looked at some more photographs. There were a few of Tarah with her husband, the man who had cheated on her. He was good-looking too, though not as tall as Radford, and he had blond hair. Kristie had never truly liked him.

Tarah's taste in men hadn't been the same as hers, another reason why it was hard to accept that she had fallen in love with Radford. It couldn't be love. Love didn't stand a chance, feeling as she did about him.

Kristie put the box on one side and went into the kitchen to make herself a cup of coffee. And remembered the time she and Radford had stood here doing exactly the same thing. Heavens, there were memories of him everywhere.

She went to bed without looking at anything else in the box. They would wait for another time. She wished she could do the same with her thoughts of Radford. Why couldn't she push them to one side too? Why did they keep intruding? Because, she told herself severely, he's a part of your life now whether you wish it or not. Jake has bound you irrevocably to him.

Jake was sufficiently improved the next day to be moved out of intensive care to a children's ward. It did Kristie's heart good to see him chatting and laughing and she didn't feel quite so bad about leaving him. Radford didn't put in an appearance at all, much to her relief, although she was told that he'd telephoned several times.

As on the night before, Kristie waited until Chloe had gone to bed before she pulled out Tarah's box. There were some beautiful pieces of jewellery, some of which she had never seen before. Were they presents from Radford? Kristie's heart sank. There she went again, thinking of him. What did it matter who they were from? Except that she might have worn some of them herself, but not if they'd been given to her by Jake's father; not in a million years. And she had no way of knowing unless she asked him, which she had no intention of doing.

At the very bottom of the box were Tarah's diaries. When she'd originally found them Kristie had been surprised because she hadn't even known that her sister kept a diary, and as she glanced through them now she felt guilty. It was like invading her privacy.

There was the break-up of her marriage—heart-rending stuff. Tarah had poured every ounce of grief into these tear-stained pages and Kristie's eyes felt moist as she read them. Her sister had put on such a brave face at the time. Kristie herself hadn't known how much she was suffering.

Suddenly Radford's name sprang out from the page.

Their first meeting. Her instant love for him. Her euphoria at having found a man she felt she could spend the rest of her life with. For months the ecstasy continued, but then the pages became smudged with tears again, everything was not going as it should.

He doesn't want children, he hates them. And he doesn't want me any more. I've seen him out with another girl. He says it's a new author but I can tell he's excited about her. I'm fed up of playing second fiddle.

The writing became more and more illegible as her tears washed away whole sentences, but Kristie managed to decipher the important words.

It's all over. He's finished with me.

So bang went Radford's declaration that Tarah had been the one to end their affair. Here was the proof. Kristie slammed the diary shut but she was too incensed now to go to bed. She wanted to speak to Radford, to confront him, and she didn't want to wait.

But of course she had to. It was almost midnight, far too late to phone him, but first thing tomorrow, she promised herself, before she went to the hospital she would ring him and tell him exactly what she thought of him and his idea of them getting wed. Not that she'd even entertained such a thing; it was a ludicrous suggestion. He'd only made it because he wanted Jake, and if he thought she couldn't see through that then he was being particularly insensitive.

In the event, Kristie didn't have to phone him; he turned up on her doorstep at half past eight the following morning. Chloe looked pleased and excited as she showed Radford into the living room where Kristie was doing some work on her computer. Chloe thought he was God's gift and would like nothing better than for the two of them to fall in love. At least she knew nothing about Radford being Jake's father, thought Kristie, or she would never have given her a minute's peace. She would have thought they were destined for each other.

'What are you doing here?' was her first blunt question as she stood up to face him. He looked awfully good in a sky-blue shirt and pale chinos. And, despite the fact that she resented every inch of him, she couldn't ignore the sudden bump of her heart.

His eyebrows rose. 'Now is that any way to greet the father of your child?'

'Shh!' Kristie looked anxiously at the doorway. 'Chloe doesn't know.'

Radford lifted his wide shoulders in an indifferent shrug. 'She'll find out soon enough.'

'Not from me, she won't.'

'Why? When we're married it will become common knowledge.' His smile held all the pleasure of a predatory animal.

'And is that why you're here?' she demanded. 'To see what my answer is? Well, I'll tell you. It's no. You don't stand a cat in hell's chance.'

His eyes glittered and narrowed on to her face. 'Is that a wise decision?'

Kristie glared. 'That sounds like a threat. I can assure you, Mr—'

'And I can assure you, Kristie,' he cut in swiftly, 'that I'll do everything within my power to get Jake. Marriage would be the simplest and least painful option but if that's out of the question then prepare yourself for battle.'

CHAPTER SIXTEEN

'OF COURSE it's out of the question,' Kristie declared fiercely. 'Why would I want to marry a liar?'

'I beg your pardon?' Radford's frown bit even deeper into his forehead.

'You lied,' she accused. 'You said that Tarah had finished with you.'

'Yes.'

'Well, I have proof that she didn't. You were the one who ended the affair.'

'Oh, yes?' The brows lifted now into his hairline.

'Yes! I've found her diaries—it's all there.'

'Then your sister was lying.'

'To her diary?' she asked incredulously. 'I don't think so.'

'Let me tell you a few things about your sister,' he said. 'Maybe you didn't know her as well as you thought.'

Kristie shot him a scornful glance. 'Nonsense. Until she moved to London we were inseparable. I know everything there is to know about Tarah.'

Radford took her hand and led her to the settee. 'Sit down and listen.'

'I will not sit down,' she fumed, snatching her hand away. 'This is my house; you have no right taking over.' But he was, whether she wanted him to or not. In truth he was taking over her body. The mere touch of his hand had set her senses sizzling and it was wrong. How could she feel like this about a man who was trying to take Jake away from her? How could she love such a man?

'Then we'll talk standing up.'

His grey eyes were steady on hers and she felt herself being pulled inexorably into their depths. She felt her whole body being taken over. This was madness, sheer madness. She shook her head and sank on to the settee—anything to break eye contact. This is your enemy, she told herself fiercely. Don't ever forget that.

Radford spoke quietly. 'I loved Tarah. When I first met her I thought I had found the girl I wanted to marry. She moved in with me. We had a lot of good times together, but then the true Tarah began to emerge.'

Kristie frowned. 'What do you mean, the true Tarah?'

'Your sister was a very possessive woman.'

'You mean she didn't like you taking other girls out,' flashed Kristie, bouncing back to her feet. She wasn't going to allow this man to say things about her sister that weren't true. 'Don't forget I've read her diary; it's all there.'

'Tarah wouldn't listen to the truth,' he told her, his mouth grim at the memories. 'She put her own interpretation on events. I was never unfaithful to her but she wasn't convinced. She wanted me to account for every second of my time. I had a third degree every evening when I arrived home. She became neurotic about it. I even caught her spying on me when I took an author out to lunch.'

Kristie couldn't accept this. He was lying; he had to be, to save his own face.

'Your sister had a split personality,' he went on. 'On the surface she was every man's dream, but the other side of her proved to be a nightmare. I'm sorry to say that, and I don't expect you to believe me, but—'

'No, I don't,' she spat. 'I'll show you her diary. You'll soon see that—'

He stopped her quickly. 'I don't want to see it.'

'Because you're afraid?'

'Because I think we ought to carry on with this discussion some other time, when you've had a chance to digest and think about what I've said. It might even be a good idea to read her diary again to make sure you weren't mistaken.' He turned towards the door. 'Perhaps I'll see you at the hospital?' he asked over his shoulder.

'Jake doesn't need you,' she flung. 'He's out of intensive care now—he's recovering well.'

'Yes, I know,' he said, swinging round to look at her.

Kristie frowned.

'I visited him last night after you'd left.'

Sheer cold horror filled her body. It would be easy for him to kidnap Jake now that he wasn't under scrutiny every minute of the day. What was she to do? Was she never going to get a minute's peace again for fear of this man?

'You surely didn't think I was going to ignore my son? I know you didn't want me there—it's why I chose to visit later. At least he was pleased to see me. I think we're developing quite a bond.' And with that parting shot he headed out of the door.

Kristie sat down before her legs buckled. A bond! Damn! What was she to do?

Marry the guy, suggested her conscience.

But I can't.

Why not?

Because he's a liar and he killed my sister.

Now you're overreacting. I thought you loved him?

I do.

Then what's your problem? Sort it out with him. Don't make a mistake you'll regret for the rest of your life.

Would she regret it? Kristie didn't know. The way she was thinking at this moment, no. But later, when she'd calmed down, when she'd had time to think rationally, what then? She shook her head. Why had life become so complicated?

All the time she was at the hospital Kristie kept looking over her shoulder for Radford. Even Jake asked where he was. 'I like him, Mummy,' he said. 'He's kind. He bought me this car.'

It was an exact replica of Radford's own car, and if Jake had told her once that Radford had given it to him he'd told her a hundred times. She was fed up with hearing it. 'He's a busy man, Jake. You can't expect him to keep visiting you.'

'Why? He can come when he finishes work. Don't you like him, Mummy?'

There must have been something in her voice. Jake was a sensitive little soul, always picking up on her moods. 'Of course I like him.' But even to her own ears it didn't sound convincing.

It wasn't until later, when she got home, that thoughts of Tarah slipped back into Kristie's mind. She sat with a glass of wine and let her thoughts wander. Chloe had gone out, thankfully, because after Radford's visit that morning she'd plied her with questions, all of which Kristie had refused to answer.

And as she leaned back and closed her eyes memories of long ago returned. Times when she and her sister were teenagers and Tarah had been in the throes of first love. She had once flown in a rage at Kristie and had accused her of trying to take her boyfriend off her, whereas Kristie had done no such thing. She'd spoken to the boy, yes, but that had been all.

There had been other occasions too when Tarah had developed irrational jealousy, moments that Kristie had completely forgotten about until now. She'd also been extremely possessive about her clothes or her jewellery, never letting Kristie borrow anything but often taking something belonging to her sister without even asking.

But Kristie had dismissed all this—sibling rivalry was part of growing up as far as she was concerned. She hadn't dreamt for one minute that Tarah had still behaved in such a manner. Could it be that Radford was right and she was wrong? But the diary? Tarah wouldn't have lied to her diary.

Urgently now, Kristie fetched it and settled back into her seat. It didn't take her long to find the page she was looking for and it took her even less time to realise that she had read into it what she had wanted to read. It was barely legible because of Tarah's tears, but she was just able to make out that it was her sister who had finished with Radford and not the other way round.

Tears filled her own eyes then and fell on the page to join those of her sister. It was a deeply emotional moment and she felt as though a release valve had been opened inside her and all the resentment and hatred that she had felt for Radford was freeing itself and flying away into infinity.

She felt sorry for her sister, sorry that she hadn't been with her at the time because then maybe Tarah would never have felt the need to lie. But grateful to Radford for insisting that she look at Tarah's diary again. *He* wasn't a liar! A smile lit her face. He was a good, honourable man who had treated her sister fairly and she owed him a huge apology.

The next two weeks in the diary were blank. Clearly Tarah had been too upset to write anything more. But then came the news:

I'm pregnant. I've finally got the better of Radford. I've got something of his that he can never take away from me.

Instead, thought Kristie sadly, Tarah's life had been taken away from her.

For the rest of the evening she felt unutterably sad, and when she went to the hospital the next day she found Radford there talking to Jake. Not that she said anything in front of her son. He was delighted to have his two favourite people visiting him at the same time.

'Mummy, Radford's brought me another car. Look, a red one. It's a Porsche.'

'You're a very lucky boy,' she told him. 'I hope you thanked him properly.'

'I did, didn't I?' asked Jake, looking up trustingly at Radford.

'You certainly did, son.'

Kristie cringed. Son! And this time he meant it. And the hardest thing was that Jake was getting attached to Radford. He'd be asking next whether he could be his daddy since Paul had disappeared from the scene. She'd actually tried ringing Paul because she felt sad that they'd parted, but he was never in and never returned her messages. And, in all honesty, it didn't surprise her. He needed to get on with his life.

When it was time for Jake to have his lunch Radford suggested they go out somewhere to eat too. 'You look as though you've been starving yourself,' he said.

How could she eat when so much was going on in her life? And she certainly didn't feel like eating now, not with Radford anyway. But she had no choice. He took her elbow and led her from the ward. 'We'll be back later, son,' he called cheerfully.

In his car Kristie's body reacted instantly to his and she knew that it would be foolish to continue fighting him now that she knew the truth. He was right—marriage was the perfect solution, both from Jake's point of view and her own. But could she be really sure that she would be doing the right thing? Wasn't Radford's main aim to get his hands on Jake? Except that he had hinted at marriage before he'd found out about his son. It was all so confusing.

They went to a hotel for their meal—Radford had booked a private dining suite. She glanced round at the elegant room, where a table for two was set near the window overlooking a lake. At the other end were plump easy chairs and a couch. 'You had this planned all along?'

'We needed somewhere to talk and not be disturbed.'

It was the 'not be disturbed' bit that made Kristie's heart flutter liked a trapped butterfly. She waited until their orders were taken and their pre-dinner drinks brought to them before she said quietly, 'I re-read Tarah's diary.'

'You did?' he asked, sipping his iced water.

'Mmm, yes,' she mumbled, not happy at having to confess to being wrong. She had perched on the edge of the couch, a fatal mistake, she realised, when Radford sat beside her.

'And?'

'You were right—she was the one who ended your affair. The page was tear-stained; it was an easy mistake.'

'So do I get an apology?' he asked with a twinkle in his eye.

Kristie was relieved to see he wasn't angry with her and she nodded. 'I truly am sorry. I should never have doubted you.'

'I guess it was natural that you would take your sister's side,' he said with a faint shrug. 'But I would never lie to you, Kristie.'

'I know that now,' she said quietly. 'I was so sure that you were the bad guy in all of this that I wouldn't have believed you if you'd sworn on the bible. Can you ever forgive me?'

'It might take a little while,' he said, but he was smiling and Kristie knew that he was teasing. She felt incredibly happy all of a sudden.

'I'm glad we've sorted it out,' she said, with the strongest urge to kiss him. Even during her periods of intense hatred she had wanted him. It was a feeling she'd buried and tried to forget, but now it rushed to the surface as though it had suddenly been mercifully released.

'I think we should drink to it.' He raised his glass. 'To a new understanding.'

'A new understanding,' she replied, wondering where that understanding was going to lead.

'What are you thinking?' Radford had seen differing emotions chase across her face. They had changed from relief to terror, which wasn't exactly what he had been hoping for. Now that she had discovered he wasn't a total reprobate he had expected a little more warmth from her. In fact, he was hoping that today would be a turning point in their relationship.

The passion was in her, he knew that; she had been so ready for him the day he had discovered she was Tarah's sister. And feelings like that didn't just go away—it wasn't something she could turn on and off at will. It was a matter now of trying to resurrect those feelings, of showing her that he cared. Perhaps he ought to tell her that he loved her so that she wouldn't think his sole reason for wanting to marry her was Jake.

There was no doubt that discovering Jake was his son had changed the way he thought about things; it had given him a new insight into life. He had a fearsome duty now. It was an awesome feeling to be responsible for someone so young. He had to be a role model for Jake, guide him through life. There were so many different aspects to think about. And he wanted Kristie at his side as he did so. She'd done such a good job so far in bringing him up that he had nothing but admiration for her.

'Jake's recovering well,' he said and was surprised to see her look suddenly fearful. 'Isn't he?' His heart stopped for a moment. 'Is there something I should know?'

'You're not having him,' she declared fiercely.

So he was right. She still thought he intended to take Jake off her. Admittedly he'd made threats but they'd all been empty ones. What he really wanted was both of them—Jake and Kristie, and he felt quietly confident that he could persuade her to marry him. If not—well, it didn't bear thinking about. Yes, he would want Jake, but he wouldn't want to hurt Kristie in the process. So they'd have to strike a deal. Hopefully, though, it would never come to that.

'I don't intend to take him off you, Kristie,' he said softly. 'How could I do that when you've made him your own?'

There was faint hope in her eyes. 'But you said—'

'I know what I said and it was wrong of me. I want us to share him, Kristie. I want you to marry me.' And, as she opened her mouth to protest, 'Please listen.'

She took a quick gulp of her wine.

'I love you, Kristie. I fell in love with you long before I knew about Jake. Probably from the first moment I met you. If it wasn't love then it was something very akin to it. Finding out what you've done for Jake, for your sister, has served only to strengthen my feelings. You're the most selfless woman I've ever met. I'm proud to love you.'

He remained silent for a moment, trying to judge her reaction. She gave nothing away. Looking at him with her huge green eyes, her expression sad almost. His heart swelled with love and he couldn't help himself. He gathered her to him, not kissing her, simply holding her against his heart.

She neither struggled nor relaxed but he could feel the pulsing beat of her. 'My sweet, Kristie,' he murmured, stroking her hair. 'I know you still have your doubts. I know you think of Tarah and the way you believed I'd treated her. It makes sense now, how much you were against me from the beginning. And I know you still perhaps think I want to take Jake from you, but nothing is further from the truth. I want us to be a family, a real family. Jake is my biological son but he's your son too in every sense of the word. He'd be happy if we married. But if you say yes, and I'm desperately hoping you will, then it must be for all the right reasons. This will be a partnership for life.'

Slowly he felt her relax, and then equally as slowly she lifted her mouth to his. Her first voluntary kiss. He felt as though he'd been given the moon and the stars and the sun all rolled into one, but he was careful to keep the kiss gentle, to take only what was offered. 'Is this your answer?' he asked gruffly. 'Is this your way of saying yes?'

'Yes,' she whispered shyly against his mouth.

Lord, she tasted so sweet, smelled so intoxicating, that he couldn't help himself. His arms tightened and his lips ground against hers in a kiss so suddenly possessive that she couldn't mistake his meaning.

Neither of them heard the door to their private room open, or the waiter silently close it again. Time and place had lost all meaning and it was a long, long time before either of them withdrew.

When they did, Kristie made one last appeal. 'It will work, won't it? You won't let me down?'

'Never,' came his strong response. 'You are my perfect woman. For all time. I love you dearly.'

'And I love you too,' she admitted. 'If I'm honest, it didn't take me long to realise that you were not the ogre Tarah painted. Although, naturally, I wouldn't admit it,' she added with a rueful smile. 'I fought for so long against my feelings. You've no idea. And now I'm tired of fighting.'

'I think we should get married straight away,' he said.

'But your sister? We can't take her excitement away from her. We must wait.'

'There you go again, thinking of others before yourself. What a sweet-natured girl you are. How incredibly lucky I am to have found you. Flick's wedding isn't until next June. I can't possibly wait that long. I want to get married now, today, tomorrow, as soon as is humanly possible. And I don't even need you to co-ordinate it—I'll make all the arrangements myself.'

'We must at least wait until Jake's better,' she insisted.

'Of course. Shall we tell him? Shall we go now?' He jumped up and pulled her to her feet.

'But our lunch?'

'Forget lunch. This is all I need.' And he kissed her again thoroughly. He was the world's happiest man.

EPILOGUE

'KRISTIE ELIZABETH SWIFT, do you take this man—'

Kristie was on cloud nine, as she had been ever since agreeing to marry Radford. She gazed into his grey eyes now, answering the Reverend's questions automatically, thinking of nothing except the fact that in a matter of minutes, seconds even, she would become Radford's wife.

All her angst had gone, all her fears, all her hatred; she was deeply in love. It was three weeks since Radford had asked her to marry him, and three weeks had never gone so quickly. His mother had been surprised, though very pleased. Felicity hadn't been surprised at all and was happy for them. She didn't even mind that they had pipped her to the post.

And Jake. Jake had been over the moon. He couldn't quite believe his good luck in finding a father. A real father. He was too young to take it all in but a real father was good enough for him.

'I now pronounce you man and wife.'

Kristie's attention was brought back to the present. This was it. This was the moment she had been waiting for.

'You may kiss the bride.'

And Radford did. Thoroughly. Right there in front of all their guests. Kristie was still on her cloud. She didn't want the kiss to stop in case she woke up and found it was all a dream. But it wasn't a dream. They held hands and they walked down the aisle, and she looked stunningly beautiful in her slender, elegant white wedding dress.

Jake walked behind, his arm still in a sling, but as proud

as Punch in his page-boy suit. 'This is my mummy and
daddy,' he said to everyone in the congregation as he
walked past. 'My real daddy.'

Everyone smiled benevolently. There were distant cous-
ins of Kristie, an aunt and an uncle, and Chloe and other
friends, but mostly they were Radford's relations. Felicity
was at the back of the church in her wheelchair and she
beamed as they reached her. 'Well done, brother,' she said.
'About time too.'

'Only because I've been waiting for the right lady,' he
returned with a grin.

'And now you've found her don't let her go,' she
warned.

'Have no fear; she's far too precious for that.' He looked
down at Kristie and smiled tenderly. 'Is this day as perfect
for you as it is for me?'

'More than perfect,' she told him softly. He looked truly
gorgeous in his grey morning suit with a green and blue
waistcoat which matched Jake's outfit exactly. As handsome a man as she could wish to meet anywhere and she
wondered how she had managed to resist him for so long.

The reception was being held at his family home, with
a firm of caterers brought in to do the honours. And, true
to his word, Radford hadn't allowed Kristie to do a thing.
He had organised it all himself, with perhaps a little help
from his mother.

They were postponing their honeymoon until Jake's arm
was better because Kristie wanted to be with him when he
had the cast taken off. They had talked about where they
would live. Radford thought they should both move into
his rooms in his mother's house until he found a place for
them somewhere nearer to London. He had told her that
she could bring Chloe with her to help look after Jake. And

so tonight that was where they would be sleeping and Kristie couldn't wait for their guests to go.

The room was enormous and decorated in dark manly colours, but it didn't detract from Kristie's happiness. She had at last found true peace. Accepting that Tarah had been the guilty party had been a hard thing to do, and she was deeply sorry that her sister had made some mistakes but not sorry that she had met Radford. Despite their rocky start, she was confident that the rest of their lives would be one big honeymoon. She loved him more deeply than she had ever imagined possible. And she said this to him now that they were finally alone.

'And I love you too, my darling,' he said as he pulled her close against him. 'More than words can say.'

She lifted her mouth eagerly for his kiss and suddenly there was no time for words. With a smile on his face and hunger in his eyes he undressed her. She wanted to do the same to him but he couldn't wait. He tore his clothes off with indecent haste and, picking her up, he carried her to his bed.

'Now, my sweet darling, I will make you truly mine.'

Kristie had no complaints as he began a slow exploration of her body. It sent every possible kind of desire screaming through her. She wanted him to hurry up and make love to her, but at the same time she luxuriated in the feelings he was managing to arouse.

There was not one inch of her that didn't pulse beneath his touch, and she could feel the heat of his body too beneath her fingertips, his hair-roughened skin, the hard muscles. Lord, he was all man. And he was hers! What a glorious thought. Hers for all time, wasn't that what he'd said? Without a doubt she would love him for ever.

'You are so beautiful, so intoxicatingly beautiful,' he muttered as his mouth closed over hers, as his body brushed against her sensitive breasts, as his fingers worked their magic in the most private part of her.

Kristie had to force air into her lungs and she wrapped her legs around him as he slowly entered her, riding with him, lifting her hips, exhilarating in every thrust he made. It was all and more than she had hoped for. Her surrender was absolute and complete.

She had never before reached such a pinnacle of ecstasy and her cries mingled with his when they climaxed at almost the same time. Their bodies shuddered and came to a slow and gradual stillness. He lay with his arm draped over her, one breast captured, his eyes closed, and Kristie lay looking at him, at this man she loved from the bottom of her heart.

'Maybe we've created another baby,' she said quietly.

The hand on her breast tightened and one eye opened. 'Would you mind?'

'Mind?' she echoed. 'I'd be delirious. Jake needs a brother.'

'Or maybe even a sister? Or perhaps one of each?' His other eye opened and he pushed himself up on one elbow. 'For a man who didn't like children I've suddenly become very fond of them. In fact—' he said, tweaking her nipple, and sending a fresh rush of sensations through her '—I think I want to spend the rest of my life making babies with you.'

Kristie grinned. 'No, sir, two's your limit, but—I have nothing against you spending the rest of your life making love to me. Would you like to do it again—now?'

And, of course, Radford said yes.

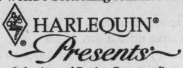

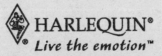

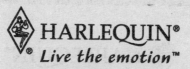

The world's bestselling romance series.

HARLEQUIN®
Presents~

Seduction and Passion Guaranteed!

THE PRINCESS BRIDES

For duty, for money...for passion!

Discover a thrilling new trilogy from a rising star of Harlequin
Presents®, Jane Porter!

Meet the Royals...

Chantal, Nicolette and Joelle are members of the blue-blooded
Ducasse family. Step inside their sophisticated and glamorous
world and watch as these beautiful princesses find they have
to marry three international playboys—for duty, for money...
and definitely for passion!

Don't miss

THE SULTAN'S BOUGHT BRIDE (#2418)
September 2004

THE GREEK'S ROYAL MISTRESS (#2424)
October 2004

THE ITALIAN'S VIRGIN PRINCESS (#2430)
November 2004

**Pick up a Harlequin Presents® novel and you will enter a world
of spine-tingling passion and provocative, tantalizing romance!**

Available wherever Harlequin books are sold.

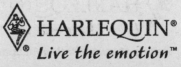

HARLEQUIN®
Live the emotion™

www.eHarlequin.com

THE WEDDING PLANNERS

Where weddings are all in a day's work!

Have you ever wondered about the women behind the scenes, the ones who make those special days happen, the ones who help to create a memory built on love that lasts forever—who, no matter how expert they are at helping others, can't quite sort out their love lives for themselves?

Meet Tara, Skye and Riana—three sisters whose jobs consist of arranging the most perfect and romantic weddings imaginable—and read how they find themselves walking down the aisle with their very own Mr. Right…!

Don't miss the THE WEDDING PLANNERS trilogy by Australian author Darcy Maguire:

A Professional Engagement HR#3801

On sale June 2004 in Harlequin Romance®!

Plus:

The Best Man's Baby, HR#3805, on sale July 2004
A Convenient Groom, HR#3809, on sale August 2004

Available at your favorite retail outlet.

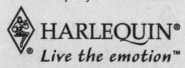

HARLEQUIN®
Live the emotion™

Visit us at www.eHarlequin.com

HRTWP

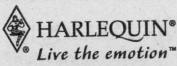

Harlequin Romance®

What happens when you suddenly discover your
happy twosome is about to be turned into a...family?

Do you panic? • Do you laugh? • Do you cry?

Or...do you get married?

The answer is all of the above—and plenty more!

Share the laughter and the tears as these unsuspecting
couples are plunged into parenthood! Whether it's a baby
on the way, or the creation of a brand-new instant family,
these men and women have no choice but to be

READY FOR BABY

When parenthood takes you by surprise!

Don't miss
The Baby Proposal #3808
by international bestselling author
Rebecca Winters
coming next month in
Harlequin Romance® books!

Wonderfully unique every time,
Rebecca Winters will take you on an
emotional roller coaster! Her powerful
stories will enthral your senses and
leave you on a romantic high!

Available wherever Harlequin books are sold.

HARLEQUIN®
Live the emotion™

www.eHarlequin.com

HRBPRW

The world's bestselling romance series.

Seduction and Passion Guaranteed!

Your dream ticket to the vacation of a lifetime!

Why not relax and allow Harlequin Presents® to whisk you away
to stunning international locations with our new miniseries...

*Where irresistible men and sophisticated women
surrender to seduction under the golden sun.*

**Don't miss this opportunity to experience glamorous
lifestyles and exotic settings in:**

This Month:
MISTRESS OF CONVENIENCE
by Penny Jordan
on sale August 2004, #2409

Coming Next Month:
IN THE ITALIAN'S BED
by Anne Mather
on sale September 2004, #2416

Don't Miss!
THE MISTRESS WIFE
by Lynne Graham
on sale November 2004, #2428

FOREIGN AFFAIRS... A world full of passion!

**Pick up a Harlequin Presents® novel and you will enter a world
of spine-tingling passion and provocative, tantalizing romance!**

Available wherever Harlequin books are sold.

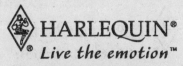

www.eHarlequin.com   HPFAUPD